THE LIVE THEATRE

THE LIVE THEATRE

AN INTRODUCTION TO THE HISTORY AND
PRACTICE OF THE STAGE

HUGH HUNT

Professor of Drama,
Manchester University

GREENWOOD PRESS, PUBLISHERS
WESTPORT, CONNECTICUT

Library of Congress Cataloging in Publication Data

Hunt, Hugh, 1911-
   The live theatre.

   Reprint of the ed. published by Oxford University
Press, London, New York.
   Includes index.
   1. Theater--History. 2. Drama--History and
criticism. I. Title.
[PN2101.H85 1978]   792'.09   78-17037
ISBN 0-313-20570-1

CONTENTS

ILLUSTRATIONS

THE NATURE OF ENTERTAINMENT

No definition can be broad enough to capture in words all that we mean by the theatre. This book does not attempt to cover all its manifestations nor explain all its techniques; but if it serves as an introduction to the full pageant of the theatre or helps others to think more deeply about its nature and practice, then its purpose is served.

When we think about what the theatre means to us, our memories of the plays we have enjoyed belong always to a particular moment of living. If we were to see those performances again, we have no certainty that we could relive the pleasure we derived from them. Our memories are of things which seemed to us right at the time; to harmonize with the moment in which they were performed—to harmonize with us personally. If we try to remember all the details of these moments of living: the scenery, the lights, the costumes and movement, the furniture and effects—the results are lifeless. A book or a poem can stay on our shelves, a picture or a piece of sculpture can be photographed, and music can be recorded, but the experience of a play is an instant recognition whose full impact can be felt only at the moment when we see it. Theatre is present, not past; drama means 'doing' not 'done'. It is what happens to us at the time of 'doing' that matters; from this experience may spring memories, but they remain memories. The moment of living has passed.

The pleasure to be derived from this experience depends upon our personal ability to associate or involve ourselves with what is happening on the stage at the moment of its happening—with its 'doing' whilst it is being done. This involvement is what we call entertainment. It cannot be provided for us by the newspaper critics, nor by the writers of books on the theatre, nor, even, by reading the text of the play. It is an active experience in which we must participate. The moment we cease to participate, the experience of theatre ceases to exist. The entertainment of the theatre depends on the ability of each playgoer to give to it, as well as to receive from it, and this action of giving on the part of the playgoer is found in a readiness to exercise his imaginative faculty. Very few people go more than once to see the same production of a play; so if, at our first visit, we are too tired to make the mental effort of participation, or if we are suffering from toothache, that particular experience will elude us for ever. What matters, then, about theatre is the immediate and personal experience it provides. The virgin imagination of a child, visiting his first pantomime, may find this experience in the sequined lady masquerading as Aladdin or the villain who sells new lamps for old. The schoolboy, who has painfully swotted his Shakespeare texts in the classroom, may find a casement opening on 'magic seas in faery lands forlorn' as he watches the heavy-handed histrionics of the amateur dramatic society. The middle-aged lady from the provinces, 'doing a show' in town, may wipe a tear from her cheek as the Prince embraces the Shop Girl, and the waltz from Act One is repeated 'pianissimo' in the background. Whilst the hardened critic with pencil poised wriggles contentedly in his stall at the obscure symbolism of the new play in the dock-side playhouse. . .

> The lunatic, the lover and the poet
> Are of imagination all compact . . .

But if this participation with the action of the play is achieved through an exercise of the imagination, we are aware—as balanced human beings—of the unreality of what we are seeing and hearing on one level of our minds—the level of our reason—whilst we experience the play's action on another level—the level of our imagination. In the mind of a child or a savage, where reason and imagination are interwoven, and the dream-world is often indistinguishable from reality, what happens on the stage may seem to be real, and the simple-minded gold-digger from the back of beyond, visiting the playhouse for the first time, may draw his gun and fire at the moustachioed villain as he pounces upon the helpless virgin. In such primary minds imagination can often overpower reason, just as it can when our minds are under great stress, or when we are in a state of great fear. But such a complete surrender of reason to imagination does not happen to the experienced playgoer; for him theatrical illusion is not delusion. When Hamlet breaks off the fight with Laertes and is treacherously wounded with the poisoned sword, we may wince or draw in our breath; we may even clutch the arm of our companion, but we are not under the delusion that any harm has been done to our favourite actor. So the tears we shed for the death of a hero in the theatre are not the bitter tears of life; and our laughter is more joyous and spontaneous because in the theatre we are not living in real life, but in theatrical life where imagination and reason exist side by side, where unreality serves as a symbol for reality. In this symbolic existence death has no sting and tears have no bitterness.

This personal involvement with a character or situation through the active use of our imagination is a form of living by proxy. Inside each one of us there are hundreds of unlived lives, of unrealized emotional experiences. When we are young we dream dreams; we imagine ourselves to be many people in many different situations: a child will imagine itself to be a tiger, an aeroplane, a Red Indian. When we are older our reason becomes stronger and our imagination becomes less active; we no longer confuse the dream with reality, but we can still identify ourselves with someone else; we can still put ourselves into their position. This process of living by proxy, or in our imagination, is far more vital in the theatre than it is in the novel, because it is being lived for us in living form.

The ardent student of the theories of Bertolt Brecht may call personal involvement with the characters or the action 'bourgeois sentimentality', for Brecht sought to correct the tendency of the fashionable theatre to smother the audience's judgement of a play's value with highly emotional 'theatricalism'. His theory of alienation attempted to create an objective approach to a play by the audience, yet no one can see *Mother Courage and Her Children* and remain objective. All art demands personal involvement, and all entertainment is ultimately subjective.

But the highest experience of theatre is achieved by those who are able, not only to identify themselves with the actors, but to value and understand the means by which the action is performed and the reason that lies behind it. The playgoer who buys his theatre as he would buy a pound of sausages—purely for its intake value—will get no more than he gives. To appreciate theatre to the full we must not only enjoy the emotions it arouses in us, but the art of creation itself.

CHAPTER ONE

THE INGREDIENTS OF THEATRE

★

IF not the oldest profession in the world, the theatre is one of the oldest. Its origins are lost in prehistoric mists and the only certainty is that its matrix or womb was religious ritual. The lost Abydos Passion Play which celebrated the death of Osiris; the liturgy of the Easter Mass out of which arose the medieval theatre; the temple origins of the Nō plays of Japan; the religious exercises which gave birth to the theatre of China; the Hindu myth which records how Brahma, the All-Father, created out of mime, song, and recitation an art which gives pleasure to eye and ear alike—these are the prototypes, the origins of the species. It was in the womb of religion and through its manifestation of ritual that the theatre was conceived.

Today amongst the Australian Aboriginals, the primitive tribes of New Guinea, and other remnants of prehistoric culture we can observe theatrical incubation taking place, as the ritual of religious magic emerges in the dance-dramas celebrating or re-enacting the tribal myths.

The matrix of religious ritual in which the theatre was originally imbedded has left upon its nature an indelible birth-mark. Religious or magic ritual is the form in which the natural world can participate in the mysteries of the supernatural. The ritual of the theatre is, then, a meeting-place between our imagination and our reason. Perfect harmony between those two aspects of our minds provides the greatest experience. The closer we get to great theatre, the more visible this ritualistic birth-mark becomes. At a great performance of *Hamlet* or *The Cherry Orchard* we can experience the same sort of elevation—the same sort of identification—with a world outside our own, as we can experience in religious ritual. The theatre becomes a temple again; the little problems of our existence fall away; we are raised above the office desk and the washing-machine; the great Gods seem to descend and move in our midst.

Clearly this birth-mark is more visible in a finely written play than it is in the commercial offerings of 'show-business', but it must also be a fine performance. We need a great deal of the child's imaginative power to turn a poor performance of *Hamlet* into a great experience for a great text does not make a great performance, and the art of the theatre is the synthesis of all its theatrical components in a perfect whole.

The involvement of the spectator in this ritual of the theatre is not necessarily achieved by an illusion of real life—that is by making everything on the stage seem as real and natural as possible. In the theatre there is no such thing as absolute reality —all is in fact illusion expressed through a ritual of performance in which the imagination is required to play a greater or smaller role. The term 'realism' in the theatre is purely relative to the degree of imaginative participation demanded by the audience.

Tyrone Guthrie, in his book, *A Life in the Theatre*,[1] has provided an apt analogy between the experience we receive in the theatre and that of religious ritual:

People do not believe that what they see or hear on the stage is 'really' happening. Action on the stage is a stylized re-enactment of real action, which is then imagined by the audience. The re-enactment is not merely an imitation but a symbol of the real thing. If I may quote this instance without irreverence, it expresses the point clearly: the priest in Holy Communion re-enacts, with imitative but symbolic gestures and in a verbal ritual, the breaking of bread and the pouring of wine. He is at this moment an actor impersonating Christ in a very solemn drama. The congregation, or audience, is under no illusion that at that moment he really *is* Christ. It should, however, participate in the ritual with sufficient fervour to be rapt, literally, 'taken out of itself', to the extent that it shares the emotion which the priest or actor is suggesting. It completes the circle of action and reaction; its function is not passive but active. This, I think, is exactly what happens to an audience at a successful theatrical performance.

[1] Hamish Hamilton, 1960.

Ritual is dependent upon faith or belief in the object of the ritual, for involvement can only operate where belief exists. In the theatre we must believe in the action. However fantastic or farcical the action of a play may be, it must be capable of involving us to such an extent that we are caught up with it, and our reason is persuaded to allow our imagination to operate. This belief in the action we call theatrical reality. Reality changes from age to age and what was acceptable reality to one age is not necessarily acceptable to the next.

Goethe, who regarded with horror the attempts of his contemporaries to introduce reality into the theatre, said:

The highest problem of any art is to produce by appearance the illusion of a higher reality. But it is a false endeavour to make this appearance so real that finally only something commonly real remains.

It would, however, be false to imagine that common reality plays no part in theatrical ritual. It is often in the most common actions, in a commonplace remark, or in a silence, that man reveals himself most clearly. Shakespeare's plays are not all poetry and Falstaff reveals himself as clearly as Hamlet. Tchekhov makes his stage as real and natural as possible, and yet we can believe in the life of his characters better than we can in the characters of Goethe. Common reality in the theatre is not a mistake, it is merely another aid to the imagination, another form of belief.

Today we are apt to decry the so-called 'theatre of illusion', and to ascribe many of the ills of our modern age to the introduction of the picture-frame arch. Yet this illusion of life being lived inside a magic box, which the theatre of illusion provides, has its time and place in the ritual of theatre; it is most required when imagination is weak, least when imagination is strong.

In the earliest forms of theatre, born in the days when wonder was still credible—when Gods came down in a shower of gold and the vertebrae of St. Madrian could cure the croup— illusions of life, which we call realistic theatre, was not required to bring about identification between the audience and the stage. The Greek theatre set in a scooped-out hollow of the hillside; its stage a circle with an altar set in the middle; its background the sky and the far-off horizon of hills; its actors disguised in weird masks and raised above human height by high-soled boots; its action interspersed by choral chants—all this carried the spectator as far away from common life as it was possible to go. The religious drama of the middle ages, with its series of stages representing heaven, hell, and the garden of Eden and as many other places as the sprawling action required, did not employ an illusion of absolute reality. The strolling players who appeared so aptly at the court of King Claudius made little use of realistic illusion to 'catch the conscience of the King'. The Chinese classical theatre requires its actors to paint their faces with weird colours, to discard all furniture and properties, and to represent their action and emotion by mime and symbolic gestures. All these are examples of ritual achieved by symbolic representation requiring a well-exercised imagination on the part of the audience.

The introduction of illusion into ritual was evolved to counter-balance the decline in the power of magic and wonder over man's mind. The society that places its faith in logic or materialism to the exclusion of belief in the supernatural eventually loses its power to use the imagination without the aid of the stimulus of illusion. It is significant that in the two societies today where logic and materialism are most urgently cultivated—Russia and the United States—theatrical illusion is most highly developed.

There are no set rules of how to mix the ritualistic ingredients of theatre so as to produce successful entertainment. Theatre is an art which depends on the personal skill of the artist. It is also a living ritual, either sacred or profane, whose object is to involve a living audience in its performance. It makes use of illusion or symbolism; it employs common or higher reality; it searches for a meeting-place of the imagination and reason of the age and society that it serves.

Before we can consider the theory and technique of the stage, we must know how the ingredients of theatre have been used in the past to achieve identification with its audience. Every crafts-man will wish to know the various uses of the material he employs, and to know the uses of theatrical material we must observe how man has used it. This is important because the history of the theatre is not so much a progression from a base mineral to a highly refined alloy, as of a kaleidoscope which reflects its ingredients in a different form. The theatre today is not better than the theatre of Aeschylus, Shakespeare, Molière, and Ibsen, nor is it necessarily worse, it is merely another arrangement of ingredients which have been used before, but which today reflect the particular imprint of their time. A revolution in the literary form of theatre, such as the new ritualistic plays of Ionesco or the new realism of Osborne, or changes of theatrical architecture, such as theatre in the round, are not new ideas, nor the destruction of old ones, they are a part of that infinite variety which throughout history has provided the patterns of the live theatre.

B

CHAPTER TWO

THE RITUAL THEATRE

THE THEATRE OF ATHENS

The Origins

'BOTH tragedy and comedy originated in a rude and unpremeditated manner, the former from the leaders of the dithyramb, the latter from those who led off the phallic songs.' This, Aristotle tells us, was how Athenian theatre began. Yet it is probable that theatre in some form or another was practised in the Mediterranean countries—certainly in Egypt and Israel and, probably, in Greece itself—before it appeared in Athens in the sixth century B.C. Of earlier manifestations and of their influence upon Athenian theatre we know nothing for certain, but Aristotle's explanation of the origins underline the principle that, wherever theatre appears, it does so as a development of a ritual.

The dithyramb, to which Aristotle ascribes the origins of tragedy, was a religious chant sung and danced by a chorus of some fifty male celebrants in honour of the god, Dionysus, or Bacchus as we more frequently call him. This ceremonial ritual was performed to the music of the pipe, and led by a soloist, or choral leader, whose part alternated with that of the chorus; thus an early form of chanted dialogue was inherent in the ritual itself as it was in the Christian Mass which gave rise to the liturgical drama of the middle ages. The word tragedy means 'goat song', and a goat was often used as a symbol of Dionysus, who was the god of fertility and harvest and so of domestic animals as well as of wine. The dithyramb was performed on a circular dancing floor; perhaps the stage was derived from the threshing floor or from the process of crushing the grapes for wine. At all events, the circular floor became the established stage for Athenian tragedy, and its name, 'orchestra', is still used in our theatres as the place for musicians.

The connexion between Dionysus and fertility explains the origins of the phallic songs from which comedy, which means 'revel song', was derived. The revellers who performed this 'comus', as it was called, wore a large phallic appendage; they stained their faces with wine or covered them with grotesque masks. It would seem that the comus was performed whilst the statue of Dionysus was being carried from his temple at Eleusis to the Athenian Acropolis, and not—like the dithyramb—on a circular stage. During this procession from which comedy sprang the spirit of the god was believed to enter into the celebrants, filling them with a god-like intoxication—though no doubt this was augmented by other means—and there seems every reason to suppose that the proceedings culminated in a thoroughly uninhibited display of the properties of fertility.

At first the leaders of both dithyramb and comus may have merely recited the myth of Dionysus, and in time this recitation may have led to an impersonation of the god himself. This rude dramatic form would eventually lead to the impersonation of other gods, demi-gods, and race heroes, but of the process of this development we know nothing for certain.

Light begins to percolate on to the scene in 535 B.C. when Pisistrastrus invited the actor-dramatist, Thespis of Icaria, to take part in the Athenian dramatic contests which were held twice a year to celebrate the festival of Dionysus. These contests took place in the theatre which we can still see today—though altered to suit Roman tastes —on the south-eastern slope of the Acropolis. We know little about Thespis, except that he is said to have written a great number of plays, that he first introduced the actor in addition to the leader of the chorus, and that he invented the tragic mask to cover the actor's face. Legend relates that he had a cart, though whether he used this as a stage to raise the actor above the chorus, or merely as a means of transport, we are not told. Other names of actor-dramatists now emerge—Choerilus, Phrynichus, and Pratinas, but their plays are lost.

In 499, the dramatic contest was won by the first dramatist

whose plays are extant—Aeschylus—of whose ninety plays, seven complete texts have been preserved. Aeschylus was born in 525 B.C. and his life spans the first half of the Athenian golden age—the age of Pericles. With the plays of Aeschylus we emerge into the full spotlight of the theatre. Before his appearance on the scene all accounts are of doubtful authenticity, and the merits of this early theatre seem to be little higher than those of elementary dance-dramas performed by savage tribes in the dim beginning of their cultural growth, but with Aeschylus we enter into the glory that was Athens—a brief glory that lasted for barely a hundred years from the victory over the Persian invaders at Marathon in 490 B.C. to the disastrous defeat of the Athenian fleet by the Spartans in 405.

The Dramatic Contests

Without the dramatic contests which were held twice a year in Athens, there would have been no plays written by Aeschylus and his fellow dramatists, for their plays were an integral part of the ritual of Dionysus worship of which the dramatic contests were the culminating ceremonial. The two major festivals of Dionysus were celebrated in Athens in January and March every year; they were known respectively as the Lenaea and the Great Dionysia. The Great Dionysia, or the City Dionysia as it was sometimes called, was the most important of the two occasions, for it was at this spring festival when the winter storms were over and the seas were open for trade that the Athenians entertained their foreign guests. Ambassadors and representatives from the allied states, as well as sightseers and pilgrims to the shrine of the fertility god, crowded the city. The whole state took a holiday; even the prisoners were released from the gaols to partake in the celebrations. Each festival lasted about a week, and in addition to the religious observances there were contests of choral chants and music, rather like the Welsh Eisteddfod. But the main feature was the three-day dramatic contest which took place in the theatre of Dionysus. Each day was devoted to a single playwright who was expected to present three tragedies and a satyr play; thus three playwrights took part at each festival, and at a later date (486 B.C.) comedies were introduced though these were more frequently performed at the Lenaea. The performances lasted all day, starting at dawn, and must have been attended by almost the entire population of the city, for the theatre held some 16,000 spectators, and contemporary accounts tell of the difficulties of obtaining seats.

The contests were regulated by the government of the city-state, and for each festival a festival director, called the Archon, was appointed to choose the playwrights and administer the rules. A script or synopsis had to be submitted by the playwrights who wished to compete and the Archon, having made his choice, provided funds from the city treasury to pay the actors for the chosen plays. The chorus and costumes, which were the most costly items in the production budget, were financed by wealthy citizens. These were known as 'choregi', and they were chosen by lot. It was considered an honour and a duty to supply the money for a chorus, and a playwright would clearly benefit from having a generous 'angel', as we call the backer of a play today. The actors, too, were assigned to the playwright by lot, and their salaries paid by the Archon, so that no influence or economic pressure could result in one playwright obtaining a better cast or a wealthier backer than his fellow contestants. The contests were adjudicated by judges chosen by lot—the prototypes of our modern critics—though public acclaim must have played a great part in the selection of the winner, as it did in the selection of the playwrights, for both the Archon and the judges were liable to severe penalties if their selection proved unpopular. Financial gain would not seem to have been the object of the contests, for although the actors, the chorus, and the playwright were paid for their services, the winners received no monetary reward, but the public honour accord-d to the successful company was considerable.

These conditions resulted in the astonishing productivity of Athenian drama, for the plays were only presented for one performance—during the early period, though later they were repeated in other cities and Aeschylus' plays were repeated after his death at the Athenian festivals. A playwright anxious to maintain his prestige as a writer was, therefore, forced to write a large number of plays.

The great period of Athenian playwriting—roughly from 500 to 400 B.C.—coincided with an heroic age. Athens was a tiny, but almost perfectly regulated society, surrounded by comparatively barbaric neighbours; many of these maintained larger armies than the Athenians and the existence of Athens was constantly threatened. As the wealth of the city-state increased, the position became increasingly dangerous. Only a strong sense of civic duty and a community united by common ideals of patriotism could maintain its defence. Patriotism was backed by a strong religious inspiration. Whilst we may smile at the confused hierarchy of gods that reigned on Mount Olympus—and the Athenians were no less amused by the conjugal complications of Zeus than we are—it was very largely the inspiration of Greek religion that maintained the idealistic aims of society. And, since national honour could not be achieved by the conquest of other lands, the idealistic impulse of the Athenians was canalized into the fields of learning and culture: the temples, the statues, the philosophy, the study of government, the plays, and the art of living were its conquests and its memorials. Thus, the outlook of society in fifth-century Athens did much to inspire the quality of the plays, whilst the public competitions ensured their quantity.

The Athenian Theatre

The origins of Athenian theatre were not dramatic, but purely choral, the performances being by a chorus and a leader. Consequently in the earliest Greek drama the chorus is the principal participant in the action. In the earliest extant tragedy of Aeschylus—*The Suppliants*—the chorus consisted of fifty members, representing the fifty daughters of King Danaus; later this number was reduced to twelve for tragedy and twenty-four for comedy. Dialogue alternated between chanting to the music of the pipe or the lyre, and spoken dialogue. Sometimes the whole chorus spoke or sang together; sometimes half the chorus was used; and sometimes lines were divided up amongst individuals. The chants were accompanied by stylized gestures and by dance.

The importance and size of the chorus resulted in the greater proportion of the stage area being given over to it. This area, the orchestra, consisted of the huge circular floor which was sixty-four feet in diameter, with wide openings on either side for entrances and exits; three-quarters of the diameter of this circle was embraced by the auditorium which rose in ascending steps around it and the whole was open to the sky; the theatre at Epidaurus is the best extant example.

Thespis is credited with the introduction of the first actor; later Aeschylus introduced a second actor, and finally Sophocles a third; but the number of actors never exceeded three during the period of the great Athenian drama. The actors were masked with larger-than-life representations of the human head, bearing fixed expressions of anguish or pride, serenity or age. By changing masks the actors were able to present more than one part in the dramas. Dumb actors and attendants were also employed, but the restriction which prevented more than three speaking actors appearing together on the stage resulted in a simplified form of action, whilst the masks themselves reduced characterization to symbolic presentation rather than life-like representation. Life-like representation was absent, too, from the dialogue which was constructed in alternating rhythms and patterns of a ritualistic nature; it was not the speech of everyday life, but of ritual drama.

The tragedies of the great Athenians were not, therefore, tragedies as we write them today, nor even as Shakespeare wrote them, they were symbolic rituals—the sublimation of an action rather than the life-like representation of it—the characters larger than life—the speech rhythmic and sometimes hypnotic in its effect.

A play written in this form can only succeed in holding an audience's attention if its action has universal significance, and if the symbol expresses a greater reality than the representation of life can reveal. The reality that Athenian tragedy reveals is the fundamental and timeless relationship of man with his destiny. The fact that the Athenian tragic playwrights were able to hold the attention of an uncomfortably seated audience, and that their plays are still able to hold our attention today is proof of the universality of their revelation.

The form and accoutrements of the stage area were at first extremely simple. There appears to have been no raised stage, though opinion on this subject is divided, and we cannot rule out the possible employment of Thespis' cart. Later, however, a long narrow stage was built at the end of the circular orchestra farthest away from the auditorium. This stage would only allow for limited movement in depth, since it was only about eight feet deep. Thus the actors and their attendants who were raised upon it (the chorus were, of course, grouped below them in the orchestra) must have appeared like the friezes we see on the Greek temples, their grouping being arranged in the form of static tableaux.

Unreality was further emphasized by the appearance of the actors, especially in tragedy where high-soled boots, huge masks, and high hair-styling raised them to a height between seven feet and seven feet six. Padding was used extensively in the costumes to give a proper proportion to these vast figures, and the whole effect must have been majestic, somewhat frightening and certainly larger than life. The high-soled boot—known as the 'cothurnus'—considerably restricted movement and added to the strangeness of these god-like beings.

As the importance of the actor increased, so the role of the chorus diminished until by the end of the fifth century it had ceased to be a major participant in the action and gradually dwindled into a musical interlude. With the increased importance of the actor and the diminishing role of the chorus, the acting areas occupied by these two elements were during the Graceo-Roman period altered in relative size. The stage moved forward and increased in depth and the orchestra became a semicircle, intead of a circle, but this happened some hundred and fifty years later than the period of the great playwrights.

The last element of the Greek theatre to be considered is the background to the acting area. This was originally a wooden hut or shed, known as the 'skêne', from whence we derive our word scene. At first there would appear to have been no permanent building. The background to a play such as Aeschylus' *Prometheus Bound* was clearly the sky and the hills, but later the plays, both comedies and tragedies, demanded a palace, a temple or a row of houses as their background. The need for the actors to make quick changes of masks and costumes also demanded a house in which to effect these changes; thus, the skêne grew in size and the stage or 'proskênion' (from which comes our word proscenium arch) was incorporated in a building which became increasingly elaborate.

About this building in the early days we know comparatively little. It had three doors leading on to the stage, and the centre door at least must have been wide enough to permit the operation of a device known as the 'ekkyclema', which appears to have been a platform or truck which was either pushed out or revolved to allow a tableau of an interior scene to be exhibited. The skêne also allowed for some form of scenery to be mounted. There were occasional demands for revolving triangular constructions, known as 'periaktoi', on each face of which a scene was painted; these were apparently mounted at each end of the stage and revolved when a new scene was required. There was a crane which raised and lowered gods often seated in chariots, and in Aristophanes' *The Clouds*, Socrates was suspended by means of this machine in a basket. An upper balcony was at some point incorporated into the façade of the skêne for gods and watchmen. There were thunder machines and lightning towers, and on the stage itself and even in the orchestra trapdoors for ghosts and descents by the actors into hell were constructed, but many of these improvements may have been introduced at a later stage of development. Argument still continues as to how all these constructions and machines were incorporated into the rigid structure of the Greek theatre, and it may be that the Greek stage was considerably more flexible than we have imagined. In the early plays, however, the demands for mechanical and visual aids to the plays, especially the tragedies, were slight. Usually the scene remained the same throughout, and if a change was required, it could be effected merely by a different positioning of the actors on the long stage. It is, therefore, fair to assume that nothing like scenery, as we know it, was employed and that the Athenian stage was a place for dramatic dialogue rather than dramatic spectacle.

The First Great Tragedies

Let us now turn briefly to a survey of the playwrights who competed in these contests. With Aeschylus' plays we enter into the full glory of Athenian civilization, and we have seen how this glory was very largely reflected in the theatrical contests, and that these contests, together with the society that designed them, were the cause of the quantity and quality of the plays, but there remains a quality in drama which is not produced by outside factors: this is the instinct of the playwright himself for dramatic writing.

When we open the first recorded play of Aeschylus, *The Suppliants*, and glance through the opening speech of the Chorus:

> Let the Lord of suppliants smile
> On our ship-borne train, who come
> From the sand-heapt mouths of Nile,
> Wafted o'er the wide sea-foam!
> Exiles from the sacred land
> Bordering Syria's meads, we flee,
> Not for guilt or murder banned
> By a people's just decree,
> But because we durst not wed
> With Aegyptus' sons, our kin,
> Hating with a holy dread
> Thought of that enforced sin . . .

we are in the presence of a dramatist, able to state his case in the first lines and to develop it dramatically to its theatrical climax, but above all knowing when to enter the story he is dramatizing. For what distinguishes the action of a play from the action of a poem or a story is the point at which dramatic action begins. Thus the story of *The Suppliants* begins in Egypt, where the daughters of Danaus are offered the choice of marriage with their cousins, the sons of Aegyptus, or death. They flee to seek the protection of Pelasgus, King of Argos, pursued by their unwanted wooers. Aeschylus with a playwright's instinct does not begin his play where the story-teller would begin it—namely, at the court of King Aegyptus, but at the moment when the protagonists arrive in Argos. Similarly Shakespeare begins

Hamlet, not at the murder of Hamlet's father, but at the marriage of his mother to the murderer. Aeschylus, like all great dramatists, knew where to begin a play and this is a knowledge which is not learnt from books; it is a feeling for dramatic material.

Perhaps it is unfair to judge the full extent of Aeschylus' tragedy from the seven texts that have come down to us, but it is probably true to say that Aeschylus was the father of tragedy, displaying an instinctive genius for drama which, if it lacked complexity of plot and subtlety of characterization, was pre-eminently right for the society and stage for which he wrote. His plays are pure tragedy, they breathe the lofty air of Olympus which transcends all human pettiness and is yet sensitive to human frailty. They raise the audience to the gods and yet purge it with terror and pity. His dramatic structures were majestic and simple, carved out of the marble of Greece itself. *Prometheus Bound*, the three plays of *The Oresteia*, *The Seven Against Thebes*, all treat of Greek gods and heroes and are impregnated with Aeschylus' pride in the origins and achievements of his race and with humility in his philosophy of ultimate submission to the gods. *The Persians*, although contemporary in subject, follows this same pattern.

To understand and appreciate this type of tragedy today we must divorce from our minds our contemporary ideas of tragedy as being something which can be suffered by every man, such as a street accident, death in a brawl, or a fatal illness. To the Greeks tragedy was not sordid, nor even sad or pathetic; it was suffering beyond human suffering—the suffering of Christ on the cross. Only the heroic soul exercising his humanity to the utmost in a noble cause can incur the wrath of the Gods and suffer more deeply than we can, precisely because he has transcended the limits prescribed for human behaviour. By this greater suffering he can wipe out his own fault or the faults of humanity. Greek tragedy is the expiation of sin, it is therefore an ennobling process. This ritual tragedy with all its horror, as immortalized by the Greeks in the figures of Prometheus, Antigone, Oedipus, and Orestes and others, was the basis upon which the plays were written. It is seen at its height in the plays of Aeschylus and

Sophocles, who still preserved something of the nature of celebrants or priests of Dionysus, the god who every year dies and is born again that man may enjoy the fruits of the earth.

In 468 B.C. when Aeschylus was at the height of his fame, the prize was wrenched from him at a dramatic contest by a playwright thirty years his junior. Sophocles, like Aeschylus, was born into the great age of Athenian culture. As a boy he had danced in the celebrations of the victory of Marathon, a battle in which Aeschylus had fought heroically, and his life, like that of Aeschylus, was lived in the age of lofty idealism. As a boy, too, he saw the great building of the Parthenon rise upon the hill of the Acropolis, and he died just in time to be spared the humiliation of Athens at the hands of her enemies in the disastrous defeat at Aegospotami. Aeschylus was made in the mould of the typical Greek hero. He was of noble parentage; he fought at Marathon, Salamis, and Plataea; he was killed in Sicily by—so it is said—an eagle dropping a tortoise on his head—an end which seems eminently in keeping with the spirit of Greek mythology.

Sophocles was the perfect example of the civilized maturity of Athens. His life was a triumph of the classical way of life; as a youth he was renowned for his physical beauty, his athletic prowess, his dancing and singing; as a man he was esteemed for his learning, his statesmanship, and his brilliance as a playwright. He won eighteen victories in the dramatic contests, won the second prize often and was never third; as an old man he was surrounded with friends and honoured by his countrymen. He died at the age of ninety and his last play, produced posthumously, displays a full maturity of style.

Between the merits of these two great dramatists—Aeschylus and Sophocles—it is difficult to judge. The greater humanity and flexibility of Sophocles' plays perhaps entitle him to a higher position as a playwright, though Aeschylus could claim the crown of the greater dramatic poet. It is, however, certain that only Shakespeare at his best can rival the plays that we still possess of these two great artists of the theatre. The plays of Sophocles that have come down to us are: *Antigone, Oedipus Rex, Oedipus at Colonus, Electra, Trachinæ, Ajax, Philoctetes,* and half of a satyr play, *Ichneutæ* (The Searching Satyrs). A comparison between Sophocles' *Electra* and Aeschylus' *Choephori* (The Libation-Bearers), which treats the Electra story, provides an interesting example of the respective merits and characters of the two great dramatists. Both plays are masterpieces, but Sophocles' play is nearer to our understanding of theatre because it contains more subtle and complex characterization. In Aeschylus' play the main character is Orestes, whose destiny it is to kill his mother, Clytemnestra, in revenge for her murder of his father, King Agamemnon. Electra, his sister, Clytemnestra, and the others are comparatively static characters. Sophocles balances his play more skilfully between the characters of Electra and Orestes, and provides a dramatically effective contrast to the steadfast and heroic protagonist (Electra) in her more feminine and timorous sister, Chrysothemis. Both plays, however, move in the rarefied air of high tragedy amongst kings and queens, princes and princesses of a semi-god-like stature; both are suitably located before the palace of Agamemnon. To understand the progress of drama from the divine to the human, we should consider a third play written on the same subject, Euripides' *Electra*. This was written eighteen years after Sophocles' *Electra*, in 413 B.C. Here the action starts, not in front of a palace, but outside a peasant's hut—the change of location is significant—where the proud Electra is married to a low-born son of the soil. She is dressed in rags and is worn down by toil. Instead of epic tragedy we find ourselves confronted by realistic tragedy; instead of pity we find pathos. Reading this play and comparing it with the rock-like quality of the two earlier dramatists, we can see how Athenian tragedy descended from Olympus to the life of the common man.

Unlike Sophocles and Aeschylus, Euripides played little part in public life. He was a rebel against the establishment and could scarcely bring himself to pay lip-service to the gods and heroes of his race. Born in 484 B.C., the productive period of his life came too late for him to be inspired by the heroic period of Athenian life; for with increasing wealth scepticism and materialism were taking the place of idealism, and the sophists were gradually arguing the gods out of existence. Euripides is sceptical, critical, doubtful of the heroic virtues, concerned more with human passions—love, hate, revenge—than with the broader issues of human destiny and divine mythology. He questions the rightness of war, exposes the injustice of the gods and the hypocrisy of the heroic idols; above all he is concerned with the passionate nature of women—Medea's lust for revenge, the fierce hatred of Electra, the devouring passion of Phaedra. His tragedies are no longer purely classical; he is the father of rationalism, if not of realism. But his realism was not a matter of form, for he retained the old ritual traditions—though he reduced the role of the chorus; it was a realism of content. His heroes and more especially his heroines are real people despite their high birth and divine ancestry. He discards the mystery surrounding the old mythological figures: Medea is a wronged woman and Jason no more than a cad. His plots, too, were more complex and lack the marmoreal simplicity of Aeschylus and Sophocles. Often his insight into character made it hard for him to fit the character into the legend, and he was forced to make extensive use of the 'deus ex machina'—the unexpected descent from heaven of a god, who puts everything to rights—in order to force the arbitrary end which the traditional story demanded.

It is significant that Euripides found greater favour with the Romans than with his contemporary Athenian audience, and through them with the playwrights of the Renaissance. He is said to have written ninety-two plays, of which seventeen have been preserved; amongst the best known today as *Medea, Alcestis, Iphigenia in Tauris, Andromache, Helen,* and *The Trojan Women.* Not all of his plays are tragedies; *Alcestis, Ion,* and *Iphigenia in Tauris* are tragi-comedies or romantic dramas with a happy ending. *Helen* is a comedy and one of his extant plays, *Cyclops,* is a satyr play.

The Satyr Plays

Before we turn from tragedy to comedy, it is necessary to say a brief word about the satyr play of which Euripides' *Cyclops* is one of the two examples that have survived. Little is known for certain about the origins of these intriguing grotesqueries which were offered as a sort of dessert after the audience had sat through the three courses of high tragedy. The plays were obviously closely related to the earliest Dionysian rites and were probably relics of some ritual older than the dithyramb and the revel song. The principal participants—the satyrs who formed the chorus—represented primitive and natural man, as opposed to the actors who represented civilized man. These semi-wild humans with their bristly hair, broad noses, pointed ears, and tails were acquisitive and curious, great drinkers of wine and completely amoral in their behaviour. The heroic characters, including the gods themselves, were brought into contact with these farcical and mischievous people led by the wine-drinking braggart, Silenus, and the resulting buffoonery becomes a skit, or 'take-off' of the ritualistic drama. It seems to us a strange exercise for serious dramatic poets like Aeschylus, Sophocles, and Euripides to undertake, but tradition demanded that these old relics of ancient mumming should round off the highly civilized offerings at the tragic contests. They help to remind us of the mysterious origins of drama and its speedy descent into popular entertainment.

The First Great Comedies

Comedy was a latecomer to the Athenian stage. Whilst it was clearly enormously popular it was never accorded equal rights with tragedy and was more frequently presented at the Lenaea festival—a more domestic occasion than the cosmopolitan Dionysia. The earliest comedies were highly topical and many of the allusions to current events and personalities would have been lost on the strangers who visited the city for the great spring festival. Old comedy, as the earliest comedies were called, retained much of the earthy character of the revel song, it was wanton, vulgar, and abounded in satire and jibes directed against living personalities; Socrates, Euripides, and the legislator Cleon were lampooned by Aristophanes. We know the names of many of the comic playwrights, and it is said that over a thousand plays were written in this early period, but only eleven comedies of Aristophanes have come down to us out of the forty which he is believed to have written. Aristophanes was born in 450 B.C. and died in 380; thus he entered the Athenian theatre towards the end of its greatest period, but, unlike his contemporary Euripides, he appears to have been a staunch conservative, bemoaning the materialism which was poisoning the old idealistic outlook. His comedies are an astonishing mixture of fantasy, obscenity, satire, and lyrical beauty.

Unlike tragedy, the subjects of Old Comedy were drawn from contemporary life and treated highly topical—often political—events. The masks of the performers sometimes bore likenesses to living personalities, though generally they were caricatures of humanity. The phallus was prominently worn—a relic of the old phallic songs—and the costume was roughly that of contemporary society. The chorus was used, as in tragedy, but often took the form of animals, birds, insects, or natural objects, as in *The Frogs, The Birds, The Wasps,* and *The Clouds.* The plots were far less closely knit than in tragedy, often no more than a stringing together of unrelated incidents around a central theme. In these circumstances it may be wondered how any dramatic effect was achieved, and yet Aristophanes wrote comedies that contain situations which not only appear genuinely funny today, but his dialogue too has a modern dramatic wit about it; he knows just how to get his laughs from the audience, as for example in this passage from *The Frogs,* which is quoted by Allardyce Nicoll in *World Drama,*[1] where Dionysus inquires of Hercules the shortest route he should follow to get to Hades:

Hercules: Just walk down to Ceramicus
Dionysus: Yes?
Hercules: Ascend the tower there—
Dionysus: All right: and then?
Hercules: Wait till they start the races down below, lean over till they give the signal to go, and then go.
Dionysus: Where?
Hercules: Over.

In *Lysistrata* he provides a genuinely comic and strangely contemporary situation in the wives who swear to refrain from

[1] George G. Harrap, 1949.

I. 'Set in a scooped-out hollow of the hillside . . .'
The theatre at Epidaurus.

2. Ritual in Performance.
Contemporary performance in Epidaurus.

intercourse with their husbands unless the latter abandon their plans to go to war. Many of his comic situations have a fantasy about them which lends his satire an unreality which is none the less pointed, for although he is often obscene from our viewpoint, Aristophanes could penetrate human frailty without brutality. Such situations as the trial of a dog for stealing a cheese, a beetle which is fed on dung in the hope that it will carry its master to heaven, or Socrates suspended in a basket, remind us of the fables of Aesop. On the whole, however, the Old Comedy, which Aristophanes and his fellow playwrights introduced, had little direct influence on the later development of comedy. It was too topical to be readily accepted by other countries to which Athenian drama was exported when new centres of learning and culture eventually took over the remnants of Athenian civilization.

By the end of the fifth century Athens no longer held its position of cultural supremacy; other city-states in Greece were beginning to build theatres and adopt the Athenian traditions and, in time, the cultural traditions of Greece were to migrate further afield—to Alexandria, to Sicily, and eventually to Rome. The disastrous Peloponnesian war reduced the power and wealth of Athens, but—worse still—it caused the gradual disintegration of the civic pride. Faith in the gods began to give way to scepticism; patriotism and idealism degenerated into materialism. The unity which had characterized Athenian democratic society was split into factions, and the scramble for individual wealth took the place of the idealistic communism in which all contributed to the general good. Under such circumstances it is no wonder that the Athenian theatre festivals ceased to inspire ritualistic writing, for faith upon which ritual depends was lacking in the new bourgeois society which dragged Zeus down from Olympus and set up Plutus, the god of wealth, in his stead.

CHAPTER THREE

RITUAL IN PERFORMANCE

SOME PROBLEMS OF PRODUCING
GREEK PLAYS

EVEN if we perform a Greek play in its original language to an audience of Greek scholars, we cannot recapture its full impact; and, in any case, we know far too little about the original methods of performance to provide more than an approximation of those methods. Greek music and dancing, which formed a considerable part of the performance, are lost to us—and, if we were to discover these arts, would our ears and our eyes accustomed to very different sounds and sights accept the antics of a Greek chorus as anything more than a museum curiosity?

In a later chapter we shall discuss the problems of interpretation of the original text in terms of contemporary theatre; it is sufficient to state here that, whatever principles we may adopt for this delicate operation of interpretation, no absolute rules and no definite formula can be given. Moreover, since the text of a play is the starting-point for all considerations of how the play is to be performed, we must face the problem that, unless we perform a Greek play in the original language, we are presented with the further complication of translation.

Translation

A translation is in itself a form of interpretation. It is conditioned by the qualities and temperament of the translator as well as by the outlook and influence of the age in which it was made. A German-speaking company faced with the problem of choosing a translation of Shakespeare may feel, with some justification, that the translations of August Wilhelm Schlegel are the most poetic and picturesque; but Schlegel was a romantic poet writing in a romantic age, and the whole feeling of his translations belongs to his own period and to the picturesque style of the theatre of that period. To be consistent, therefore, a Schlegel translation should be performed in the costumes, scenery, and acting style of the early nineteenth century.

Most of our translations of Greek plays are more contemporary than Schlegel's, but many of them regrettably adopt an archaic style, related neither to the Greek nor to the contemporary theatre. This archaic style is more damaging to comedy than to tragedy, where ritual assumes greater importance and where a more ritualistic language is required. If we wish Greek comedy to provide entertainment, we must first be sure that the translation is in tune with the speech of our age. A Greek comedy translated into eighteenth-century English and performed in the style of twentieth-century theatre can result in a hybrid performance whose style is related neither to the author nor to the audience. It is the duty of the interpreter of a Greek play to keep the lines of contact between the original and the contemporary as direct as possible, so that interpretation, however liberal, is made directly from one language to another and from one age to another. By language is implied, not merely the translation of words, but of rhythms, expressions, and speech mannerisms.

The comedies, more especially those of Aristophanes, depended for much of their humour upon topicality. This topicality extended not only to the lampooning of living and recognizable characters, such as Euripides, Socrates, and Cleon, but to the parody of language, rhythms, and expressions.

In *The Thesmophoriazusae*, for instance, the tragic style of Euripides is parodied, and in *The Frogs* the verbal sophisms of the philosophers are lampooned. Clearly much of this verbal parody will be lost upon a modern audience; some of it can with skill be translated in a form which indicates a timeless humour, but much will, of necessity, have to be cut. But even satire which was aimed at a particular personality or at a social or political target can be humorous today, providing the personality is a recognizable type of humanity and the target a timeless form of human foolishness. Thus a play such as *The Lysistrata* can surprise us with the basic relevance of its characters, outlook, and situations, providing archaism for its own sake is avoided.

Clearly greater liberties can be taken in translation of comedy than are required or permissible in tragedy. How far can these liberties be stretched? Can we, for instance, legitimately alter the text to embrace a contemporary situation, change the characters into their contemporary equivalents, eradicate archaic references which do not suit these alterations, and substitute machine guns for spears? The reply depends on whether we intend to translate or to adapt the play, for between translation and adaptation there is a complete difference of outlook. This difference concerns first the style of the play. A translation should seek to preserve the style by translating it into the nearest contemporary equivalent; the primary object of an adaptation is to alter the original to suit contemporary taste or to hit a contemporary target. Secondly, the relationship between the audience and the performance is altered in an adaptation. Once the audience is aware that it is not seeing the genuine article, nor even an honest attempt to reproduce that article, the particular pleasure that is derived from the feeling of contact with the past is lost. Contact with our roots, which no doubt the psychologists can explain, is a sensation which provides excitement and pleasure; and, whilst we may not worship our ancestors, as the Greeks did, we are aware of the desire to break down the time barrier and re-live the past. Even a child, once aware of history, imagines and re-enacts it. So the nearer we can translate the original to the contemporary, and the less adaptation we interpose, the greater will be the effect of the former upon the latter.

This does not deny liberty of interpretation to the translator. It would be wrong to state that any of the alterations mentioned earlier are destructive in principle; anachronism does not destroy the past-present relationship, as Shakespeare and, indeed, all the poets and painters of the pre-archaeological age have shown. Anachronism was, in fact, a useful method of conveying the past to the present in a recognizable form. But anachronism depends on the audience accepting the conventions used. The task of the interpreter of a Greek play is to assess that acceptance, and this inevitably involves a delicate and personal judgement of how far a translation can be stretched without damage to the past-present relationship. We can, therefore, place no exact limits on the legitimate liberties of the translator, other than the imperative of retaining contact between the original author and the contemporary audience; and, whilst tragedy demands greater adherence to the ritual of the text than does comedy, both demand a rigid adherence to a ritualistic style.

The Acting of the Comedies

In Greek comedy this adherence to ritualistic style will be mainly found in the feeling of the performance rather than in the language; for, whilst the ritualistic nature of Greek tragedy demands a formal style of acting which includes the language, Greek comedy demands a far looser acting style and a more personal relationship with the audience.

In comedy generally, and in Greek comedy in particular, the contact between actor and audience is essential to the intention and nature of the plays. This contact is made by the ability of the actor to coax his audience into a frame of mind in which it can share the joke with him. It demands from the actor a 'comedy point of view', about the part he is playing.

Athene Seyler in *The Craft of Comedy*[1] explains that a 'comedy point of view' is a state of mind in which the comic actor, unlike the dramatic actor, stands slightly outside the character he represents and endeavours to point out his delight in some aspect of that character to his audience. This process of sharing a comic experience must depend upon the sense of humour of both actor and audience, it follows that the acting of comedy is a far more individual process than the acting of tragedy; and, whereas a poor tragedian may be just acceptable to an audience, a poor comedian will quickly collect the rotten eggs.

This 'comedy point of view' not only embraces a state of mind in which an actor delights in sharing his point of view with an

[1] Frederick Muller, 1943.

audience, it also demands that the actor is able to see the truth
of the character he is presenting and to distort it or upset its
balance so that it appears to be comic. If there is no basic truth
in the character presented or if its interpretation by the actor
fails to absorb that truth, then distortion has no point from which
comedy can spring. In the case of Greek comedy distortion of the
truth often takes the form of the purely absurd. But even in
absurd comedy, such as we find today in the plays of N. F.
Simpson, the truth of the character must be found before
distortion can take place.

The most distinctive feature of the distortion required in
Greek comedy is that, whereas in artificial and high comedy the
distortion of truth is a distortion of outlook and behaviour, in
Greek comedy it is also a physical distortion.

We have already referred to the grotesque masks of the comic
actors and to their custom of adorning themselves with a phallus
of exaggerated proportions. Exaggeration was also apparent in
their costumes and, no doubt, in their antics. Thus the performance of the Greek comic actor was closer to that of the modern
clown than to the polite behaviour of the contemporary actors in
the comedies of Noël Coward or Oscar Wilde. How far the contemporary performer of a Greek comedy should go in the distortion of his physical appearance is perhaps a matter of taste,
but clearly some degree of physical distortion is required if we are
to interpret the ritualistic style of the original. To dress our
actors in an exact reproduction of Greek comic costume may be
offensive to our ideas of good taste, but better that than to destroy
the ritual of the original by dressing them as handsome citizens of
Athens straight out of a picture by Alma Tadema.

Grotesque costume demands grotesque acting and the latter
is essential in grotesque situations. The situations in the comedies
of Aristophanes are grotesque and highly improbable. Their
nearest equivalent is to be found in the improvised comedy of
the Italian Commedia del'Arte, where again we find distorted
masks and fantasticated costume used.

In the Italian comedy, whose ancestry can be traced back to
the Roman mimes—if not further—the text was not written;

only the situations, the argument, and the main lines of character were fixed. It was the duty of the actor to provide such words as were necessary and, above all, to provide his particular grotesque interpretation of the character. This tradition stretches down to the modern clown with his mask-like make-up and his exaggerated costume and to the red-nosed music-hall comedian. It is in this ritualistic style of acting, or, if you prefer it, clowning, that we may find an approach to the performance of Greek comedy; for here, and here only in the modern theatre, can we rediscover that sense of timeless parody of man's foolishness, absurdity and essential loveableness that characterizes the ritual of Aristophanes' comedy.

The Staging of Greek Tragedy

When we turn to the interpretation of the tragedies of Aeschylus, Sophocles, and Euripides we are, or should be, largely concerned with the question of architecture—the architecture of the plays and of their staging. The tragedies are not, like the comedies, concerned with topical parody, but with eternal values, and their structure has the same architectural quality as we find in the symmetry and proportions of the theatres themselves. We should, therefore, no more think of altering this symmetry to convey the spirit of tragedy to a contemporary public than we should think of modernizing the Theatre of Epidaurus.

A Greek tragedy is a literary architectural construction written for a physical architectural construction, yet like all great art its message belongs both to its own and to all time. Its power to move us lies in the harmony of the three elements of text, ritual, and theatre. Here then lies our problem; for, whilst we can see the greatness of the original text, its architectural features of ritual and theatre are, in part, hidden from us. How, for instance, did the chorus move and function? What was the music that accompanied it? What was the physical relationship between the chorus and the actors? What form of stage stood in front of the skêne façade, and how did that curious device, the ekkyclema, work when it revealed the interior of a building? It may be that all these lost conventions and devices would seem childish or merely archaic to us, but until the answers are known the director and scene designer of a Greek tragedy will always feel frustrated when they approach the problems of interpretation into a modern idiom, for interpretation, however widely it differs from the original, must first absorb the relevant factors of the original.

In the case of the Greek theatre our lack of knowledge of certain vital features is made more frustrating than it is in the Elizabethan playhouse; for whereas in the latter case the theatres have been totally destroyed and all we possess is a crude and highly inaccurate drawing, in the case of the Greek theatres we can still see a substantial part of the original buildings; and what remains of these mighty structures makes us desire to know a great deal more about them. Moreover, whereas the original architecture and functioning of the Elizabethan playhouse has no important bearing on contemporary interpretation, the Greek theatre and its functioning has a considerable bearing on our approach to the ritual of Greek tragedy. In approaching the problem of ritual, we must endeavour to create our own ritual, even if our creation be founded on little more than our own imagination; for there is a primary need to transmit to a contemporary audience what we might call the elevation of Greek tragedy; its majesty which demands space and proportion; its dignity which demands solemnity of movement and gesture; not least its tactile properties, by which is meant the materials out of which its scenery and costumes are constructed. We cannot produce Greek tragedy successfully in the village hall, and if we are forced to produce it in a proscenium arch theatre, then Reinhardt was right to demand that his production of *Oedipus Rex* with John Martin-Harvey in 1912 should take place in the Royal Opera House, Covent Garden, which at least provided some degree of architectural majesty to match the ritual solemnity of the text. But obviously a proscenium theatre—a theatre of illusion—is far from ideal and presents us with the necessity of making a whole series of compromises. Ideally we want an open-air Greek type of auditorium, not only because the circular formation is associated in our minds and, perhaps in our deeper sub-conscious minds, with magic and ritual, but because the

Greek form allows the audience to view the performance from above. The productions of the old tragedies by the Greek National Theatre in the great theatres of Athens, Delphi, and Epidaurus, or the productions given seasonally in the ancient theatres at Taormina in Sicily and at Orange and Aix en Provence have an advantage over anything we can produce in our colder and less reliable climate, unless we are fortunate enough to produce them in a roofed-in open stage with a Greek auditorium, like Stratford, Ontario, where Tyrone Guthrie produced *Oedipus Rex* with James Mason in 1954.

One of the compromises demanded by the proscenium arch theatre will inevitably affect the chorus; for the tragic chorus was required to form geometric patterns to the accompaniment of music whilst speaking or chanting the choral odes. As with the counter-marching of a military band or a gymnastic display, such patterns are only effective when seen from above. If, therefore, we have to manœuvre our chorus in a typical proscenium theatre, where a major part of the audience is seated below the stage level, we are bound to lose much of the effect of patterned movement. In whatever type of theatre we perform we must strive to achieve form and proportion in spatial arrangement and this applies no less to the actors and chorus than to the setting. Like good sculpture, a Greek tragedy requires to be shown off in space. A modern production, therefore, needs a setting which conveys the feeling of the open-air hillside theatre. It is difficult to convey this feeling with the use of illusionary scenery—painted backcloths representing a panoramic view of the Greek landscape and flimsy flats which shake every time the palace doors are opened or closed. Abstract design and the play of light on solid three-dimensional surfaces are closer to the elemental style we are seeking, but the best answer will always be found in the Greek theatre itself.

Padded costumes, masks, and the high-soled cothurnus for the actors are, perhaps, not essential, but their employment will help to convey the larger-than-life feeling of the mythological action and, more important still, they will oblige the actor to resist any temptation to adopt a naturalistic approach and may lead him to the discovery of the old epic style which is lost to the contemporary stage.

To discover this style the actor must first adopt an approach to the part he is playing which is largely different from the approach he would make to a character in Shakespeare's plays and totally different from his approach to the characters of naturalistic theatre.

The high persons of Greek tragedy, whilst their actions may represent the actions of real people who lived, or were believed to have lived, are not presented as real people. They are, rather abstract images of real people, just as Henry Moore's figures are. The actor must, therefore, achieve detachment from the character; he must present the passion of Oedipus, not be Oedipus. Classical detachment which is the basis of the old epic style does not allow for personal indulgence in passion, nor for the extraneous ornamentation of character. The passion must be pure, the presentation of character must be symmetrical, the development must be harmonious with the action. Such requirements are easier to define by reference to their abuses than to their virtues. It is easy to see that an actor who tries to invent an original character for Oedipus will fail to fulfil the requirements; so, too, will the actor who uses the part as a virtuoso performance of his own histrionic powers. It is less easy to define how an actor can project passion without personal indulgence, character without extraneous invention, and symmetry and harmony without becoming merely an automaton. Yet passion can be individually expressed apart from character, as any student of acting knows, and harmony and symmetry can be achieved without loss of individual art. In this abstract form, divorced from the many distractions of common reality, the character becomes a symbol for all humanity, not merely a character fixed in time and space. Thus, the epic characters of Aeschylus' *Oresteia* belong to a higher reality, whereas the domestic characters of O'Neill's *Mourning becomes Electra* belong to a common reality and the whole approach to the staging and acting of the two plays requires an understanding of the style of each. The action of Greek tragedy is not concerned with domestic or private events, but with universal and public events; it may be that we can no longer see these history plays as public events in the same way as a Greek audience was able to do, nor hold these high persons in the same awe, but we can recognize in the action of these tragedies the eternal ritual of human nature and in the high persons we should find the struggle between the elemental forces of humanity awe-inspiring precisely because it is divorced from the commonplace and the particular.

It could be argued that the chorus of some of the tragedies, though not of all, represents more directly the attitude of the common man towards the events of the action. This argument can lead to a false conclusion—namely, that the chorus should, therefore, be made to appear as natural as possible. The chorus of the tragedies is not only concerned with the reactions or emotions of an audience, sometimes it was used, as we use scenery and lighting today, to provide atmosphere, relief, and contrast, or to set the scene for the action. On other occasions the chorus was used as an active participant as in the *Eumenides* and the *Suppliants*. The reactions and emotions of the chorus, whether they express the feelings of the audience or not, are corporate expressions. They are not a collection of individual Athenian citizens or of fifty different daughters of King Danaus, but a corporate and almost disembodied character. They are, in fact, emotions and expressions divorced from personalities. We cannot, therefore, treat the chorus as we would treat the crowd in *Julius Caesar* or the strikers in Galsworthy's *Strife*. The more abstract and less personal the chorus is, the more powerful its effect on the action.

The chorus should, therefore, be masked, even if the high persons are not; it should be dressed in uniform costume, move in rhythmical forms, use corporate gesture and, whilst it may not be desirable for the chorus to chant, it is highly undesirable to allow it to chat. Only by preserving the anonymity of the chorus can we avoid being side-tracked into the historical naturalism so dear to nineteenth-century tradition.

The treatment of the chorus in Michel St. Denis's production of *Oedipus* in 1945 and the even more striking treatment used by the same director in the production of Stravinsky's opera-oratorio of *Oedipus* in 1960 achieved this abstract quality. In the latter production this effect was achieved in a style which was con-temporary in feeling, whilst preserving a direct link with the past. The task of the director and of all creative interpretation in relation to plays of the past must always be to bring the play to life without sacrifice of the author's intention and without archaism which destroys its impact on a live audience. This is the problem which confronts the stage-artist, be he actor, director, or designer, in the approach to the ritual theatre of Greece. The solution of this problem in terms of personal artistic expression is what we mean by the live theatre.

CHAPTER FOUR

THE SECULAR THEATRE

NEW COMEDY AND THE ROMAN THEATRE

Menander and New Comedy

THE Hellenistic period which followed the Athenian cultural ascendancy was mainly characterized in Greek theatrical history by the growth of new theatres in cities outside Athens and by their architectural development, as well as by the gradual ascendancy of the actor over the playwright. Divorced from the full religious background of the Athenian ritual of the fifth century, the theatres gradually became places of entertainment. This had two major consequences: first, comedy began to assume ascendancy over tragedy; secondly, the theatres themselves became places for action rather than symbolism. The architectural development of the theatres was mostly concerned with the stage area. Probably many of the machines, such as the periaktoi, the trapdoors, and upper stories or balconies, were introduced or perfected during this period. The development of the stage involved the reduction of the orchestra which assumed the semicircular shape that we see in most of the old ruins today. The actors rather than the authors began to assume the leadership of the stage, with the result that the theatres became increasingly places for spectacular display or for highly 'theatrical' performances—a tendency that Aristotle in his *Poetics* deplored. The Guild of Dionysus was the first actors' trades union, and obtained remarkable privileges for actors, including exemption from military service, freedom from arrest, and special travel facilities. Under Alexander the Great, actors became important state officials and were sometimes used to carry out delicate diplomatic missions. Aristophanes' highly individual and topical comedy was not entirely suitable for the other cities of Greece which were now building theatres, and a new comedy came into being which proved to be a more exportable type of drama: a more realistic comedy took the place of the grotesque situations and of the caricatures which depended on knowledge of Athenian personalities and current topics. The plots of the new comedy were more succinct and universal; love themes and sentiment replaced the old boisterous farce.

Of the many writers of this new type of comedy whose names are known to us only about four thousand lines of the playwright, Menander, and one complete recently discovered play, *Dyscolos* (The Peevish Man), have been preserved. For the rest we have to deduce the type of comedy they wrote from the statuettes of contemporary actors and the vase paintings of theatrical scenes. Menander lived from about 342 to 292 B.C. Enough of his work remains to indicate that he was an observant and considerable dramatist. Whilst his imaginative range was much narrower than that of Aristophanes, he was better able to construct a dramatic plot and his comedies provided rich material for future playwrights.

In Menander's plays the chorus takes practically no part in the action and the actor is predominant. His themes are realistic stories of city life; he deals with the intrigue, the manners, the domestic life of the city. His characters are easily recognized types of citizens—gossips, stupid slaves, cooks, musicians, young wives married to old husbands, and above all, courtesans. In his comedies we are in the presence of the day-to-day life of a bourgeois Athens stripped of its high idealism. *Samia* (The Girl from Samos) treats romantic love and its many misunderstandings; *Perikeiromene* (The Girl with the Shorn Hair) tells the story of twins abandoned in infancy and later reunited—a tale that was to find great favour amongst Roman dramatists and later adopted by the English Renaissance. *Epitropontes* (The Arbitration) mixed laughter with pathos in a recipe which is almost modern. Just as Euripides' tragedies are not pure classical tragedy, so Menander's comedies are not purely classical in feeling. Comedy becomes mixed with romance and with romance came a close observation of contemporary manners. Thus, his plays provided the future model for comedy just as Euripides' tragedies had done for the future of tragic drama.

The Origins of Roman Theatre

From Menander onwards the spotlight passes from Greece to Rome, for in 270 B.C. the Roman legions conquered the Greek city of Tarentum, thus opening the gates of Rome—the Rome of stern republican virtue, martial prowess, and good business sense—to the softening influence of Greek art. It would, however, be a mistake to attribute the origin of Roman theatre solely to late Greek or Hellenistic influences; for Etruscan influence played a significant role in the development of the theatre, as it did in other aspects of Roman life and art. It would appear that a crude form of theatrical performance, known as the Fescinni verses, developed in Etruria almost simultaneously with the earliest period of Athenian plays. Like the phallic songs and dances of Athenian comedy, these primitive ritual verses were connected with fertility rites and were probably performed at marriage ceremonies. Their origin may have been Athenian or may have sprung from similar circumstances and conditions. As early as 364 B.C. a company of Etruscan actors appeared in the circus Maximus in Rome as part of the Roman Games.

Folk players performed in Sicily, too, known as the Phlyakes, though these may well have been of Athenian colonial origin, perhaps springing from the Satyr plays. These farces were performed on a raised wooden stage without a chorus, their performance was largely improvised and took the form of slapstick burlesque of the old myths, in which the gods were dragged down to a farcical level: Zeus appears as the lover climbing into his lady-love's chamber by means of a ladder; Apollo is frightened by the brutal Hercules. These supernatural beings mingled on equal terms with stock characters such as the foolish old men, and the stupid slaves as portrayed by Menander.

From Sicily the folk plays or mimes moved north to Paestum and to Atella, where they became more literary. The characters assumed stock names such as Bucco, the stupid slave, the senile old man—Pappos, the greedy man—Maccus, and from Atella they came to Rome. These crude mimes—the Atellan mimes as they are called—though they have no literary or dramatic value today and little is known about their performance, are significant in the story of the Roman theatre, not only because they influenced the written comedies, but because they eventually outlasted them. Their unpretentious nature and their lack of literary form gave them greater flexibility than the established theatre. They were able to adapt themselves easily to changes of fashion and to elude the persecutions of church and state. The mimes were essentially popular drama, belonging to the market-place rather than to the theatre buildings, and, as such, less subject to political and social upheaval; and when Rome fell and her great theatres were pulled down by the Vandals and the Goths, the little Atellan mimes lived on, wending their way through Europe under the name of the Commedia del'Arte, to hand their colourful and essentially earthy tradition to later ages.

The Roman Playwrights

When Tarentum fell to the Romans, its Greek actors moved northwards and with them came, in the year 240, Livius Andronicus, who adapted and presented two Greek plays in Latin—a comedy and a tragedy—at the festival of the Roman Games. From then onwards theatrical performances were regularly given at the Roman festivals and the Roman theatre was committed to imitation and adaptation of the Greek. But, though Greece provided the major influence, the spirit of Roman theatre was a sad and debased reflection of its idealisms, reflecting the different outlook of the two societies. Under the sterner and more disciplined society of the early Roman Republic, Greek tragedy was just acceptable, but comedy in the manner of Menander was the major theatrical fashion.

Plautus (254-184 B.C.), drawing on Menander for his plots and on the mimes for his farcical incidents, provided a number of comedies which reflected the teeming city life and the less virtuous side of Roman republican society. His aim was frankly

3.*a* The Theatre of Massive Spectacles.
Reconstruction of the theatre at Orange.

3.*b* 'All that remains . . . is stones.'
The theatre at Orange today.

4. The Pageant Theatre.
The cart of the Nativity from *The Triumph of Isabella* (1615).

popular, mixing sentiment with farce: domestic intrigue revolving around the dominance of the Roman matron, the faithless husband and the courtesan. The triumph of love was Plautus' theme, but above all his comedies reflected the money-conscious materialism of Roman society. His plots were to provide the basis of many comedies in later ages: in *Aulularia* he portrayed a miser, Euclio, who was later to reappear as Harpagon in Molière's *The Miser*; in the *Menœchmi*, he restated Menander's play of the twins which was later to be adopted by Shakespeare in *The Comedy of Errors*; in *Miles Gloriosus*, he provided the model for Falstaff, and in *Rudens* the character of the shipwrecked Marina was to find its echo in Shakespeare. Thus Plautus acts as a bridge between Greek comedy and the later comedies of the European theatre, for in England and France it was Latin rather than Greek that was the more popular study in the schools.

Terence (195 B.C.–A.D.159) was to provide an even stronger influence on future European comedy, for, being a more literary playwright, his plays were more closely studied by the grammarians of the Renaissance and were widely read in the schools and universities. His model was almost exclusively Menander; indeed Caesar nicknamed him 'Demidiate Menander' (half Menander). His plays were aimed at a more sophisticated audience than those of Plautus and in the noisy, brash society of Imperial Rome it is doubtful if he found much favour outside the narrow circle of the literary clique. Six of his plays are extant: *Andria* (The Girl from Andros), *Hacyra* (The Step-Mother), *Heauton-timorumenos* (The Self-Tormentor), *Eunuchus* (The Eunuch), *Phormio* and *Adelphi* (The Brothers). His central character is nearly always the well-bred young Roman: witty, delighting in epigram, and opposed by the stupidities of old age. This character became the model for the gallant of the French classical theatre and of the English Restoration comedy.

Even less popular in his own day, but just as influential in the future, was the only significant Roman tragic playwright, Seneca, who committed suicide by order of Nero in A.D.55. Seneca's plays were probably never acted on the stage in his lifetime, but were widely read in literary salons. Just as Plautus and Terence

D

followed the style of Menander, so Seneca followed Euripides. His subjects were mainly the old Greek mythological stories: *Medea, Oedipus, Phaedra, Agamemnon, Hercules Furens*. But whilst he borrowed his plots and especially his sensational incidents from Euripides, he discarded his rationalism and his psychological realism. He delighted in bloody murders, in torment, and in the atmosphere of pervading doom. His plays are dark and gloomy affairs, filled with bombast and rhetoric. In them we foresee not only the atmosphere, but often the thought of Elizabethan, Jacobean and French classical tragedy.

> Fall now this mighty house of famous Pelops,
> And crush me, so it crush my brother too.
> Come dare, my heart, a crime no age shall pardon
> But no age e'er forget. Venture some deed
> Bloody and fell such as my brother would
> Wish to be his.

These lines might have been written by Marlowe, Webster, or Corneille.

By discarding the chorus, or reducing it to a mere musical interlude, and by dividing their plays into five acts, Terence and Seneca set the play form which lasted down to the twentieth century. Their importance lies not so much in the literary or dramatic value of what they wrote, as in their transmission of ideas and forms from the Greek to the European theatre.

Roman Showmanship

But the characteristic theatre of Rome was not the theatre of the literary dramatists, but the theatre of massive spectacles. Although Greek tragedies were translated and presented in the last two centuries before Christ, the polyglot society of the Roman Empire was not interested in the ritual culture of Athens, but only in the bloody incidents and melodramatic events which occurred in the old myths; these events the Greeks had kept in the background of their theatre, usually relating them by means of a messenger rather than by direct representation. Even in the early days of the Roman republic, Greek tragedies were adapted to show more action and spectacle. The architectural form of the theatre was altered too, to suit the imperial taste for extravagance and display. In 55 B.C. the first stone theatre was built by Pompey; its stage was 300 feet long and scenery was more extensively used than in Greece. The skêne was embellished with pillars, statues, gilded wood, coloured marble, and glass panels; a vast gilded roof jutted out over the stage, and the auditorium seated 40,000 spectators. The shape of the auditorium remained substantially the same as in the Greek theatre, though it was reduced to an exact semicircle; the orchestra, now also a semicircle enclosed by the auditorium, was used to seat the privileged spectators. But the most significant change was in the façade of the skêne which became a huge, ornately decorated wall, resplendent with pillars and statues, pierced by three vast doors and incorporating a wide and deep stage on which hundreds of performers could appear and move. The whole theatre building was enclosed within high walls, and although there was no roof over the audience, awnings of coloured linen, attached to masts fixed in the containing walls, could, if necessary, be drawn to protect the public from the sun. The Roman theatre was, in fact, an enclosed theatre, rather than an open place for acting. Even a front curtain was introduced in later Roman theatre. This was pulled upwards from a trough in front of the stage, instead of descending from above, as it does in our modern theatres. The main purpose of these vast palaces was clearly to present spectacle rather than spoken drama.

Some idea of spectacular performances under the Empire can be gleaned from a contemporary account of the opening of Pompey's theatre when five hundred mules, three thousand elephants and giraffes processed across the stage representing the trophies of fallen Troy. But worse excesses were to come, for the Roman theatre under Nero, like the Elizabethan playhouses, had to compete for popularity with the wild beast hunts, sea fights, gladiatorial combats, chariot races and the ever-popular sport of watching Christians being torn to pieces by lions. The theatre managers, like their descendants in later ages, were undaunted by this competition. They managed to give the public what it wanted. Realistic battles staged by squadrons of cavalry, thousands of captives borrowed from a conqueror's triumph, slaves bearing the trophies of some sacked city, gold statues and costly hangings torn from the temples of Athens or Alexandria, real kings in chains, slave girls raped in public, criminals handed over by the state to be executed, decked out a Roman holiday in the theatre. Nothing that Hollywood has so far conceived could match the excesses of the Roman 'spectaculars'.

It is hard to imagine how a play could be performed in the midst of such tumult, and yet the Roman actors and actresses—for women were now admitted to the stage—still acted debased adaptations of the old Greek plays, dressed in the masks and padded costumes of their Athenian predecessors. It is hardly surprising that the profession of acting was mostly confined to slaves and prostitutes, but these could rise to high honour and earn enormous salaries, if Pliny is correct in saying that the great Roman actor, Roscius, earned fifty million sesterces (half a million pounds in our money) a year. He was awarded a gold ring —the equivalent of being knighted—by Sulla.

Theatres were a valuable instrument of government. Not only were they used to enhance the prestige of the Imperial city in the eyes of its conquered peoples by an impressive display of wealth, but to keep the public mind off other matters. Public discontent over an unpopular war, heavy taxation, or the failure of domestic policy could be smoothed over by a theatrical orgy. Candidates for imperial power and popular favour found the expenditure of a few million sesterces on these vast entertainments brought a worth-while return in votes. This policy was found valid not only in Rome, but throughout the Roman world, and theatres were built throughout the Empire. Today we can see the vast remains of the colonial theatres in Provence as well as in Asia Minor, North Africa, and at Verulamium (St. Albans) in Britain.

Never before and never since has such a vast amount of money been poured into the theatre with less enduring results. With the exception of the plays of Plautus, Terence, and Seneca, all that remains of the Roman theatre is stones. It was debased by its spectacle and finally destroyed, not only by the decline and fall of the Roman Empire, but by the constant hostility of the Christian church. When Christianity eventually became the dominant religion the theatre was gradually beaten to its knees, for no Christian could be an actor under pain of excommunication and devout Christians refrained from attending the theatre. Sunday performances were forbidden and eventually in the sixth century A.D. the Roman theatres were closed. So religion which had been the womb of theatre decreed its death. The child to which religious ritual had given birth had grown into a monster which threatened the whole structure of social and religious life. Tertullian in his treatise, *De Spectaculis*, urged Christians to satisfy their desire for spectacle by participating in the ritual of the Christian church. Little did he foresee that in time that ritual would give birth to another theatre. So, for four hundred years the theatre died, and only the little carts of Thespis carried their crude mimes round the back streets of Europe, keeping alive the old instinct for acting until time had purged the horrible excesses of Roman showmanship from the memory of man. In the course of theatrical history this ever present temptation to use the theatre for vulgar display has more than once decreed its death; for theatre contains within itself the seeds of its own decay, and the danger of the ascendancy of vulgarity in a medium which must always be popular is as present today as it was in the Roman Empire.

CHAPTER FIVE

THE PAGEANT THEATRE

LITURGICAL PLAYS AND THE RELIGIOUS CYCLES

Christian Liturgical Drama

'WHILST the third lesson is being chanted, let four brethren vest themselves. Let one of these, dressed in an alb, enter as though to take part in the service, and let him approach the sepulchre without attracting attention and sit there quietly with a palm in his hand. Whilst the third response is chanted, let the remaining three follow, vested in copes, bearing in their hands incense-burners, and stepping delicately, as those who seek something, approach the sepulchre. These things are done in imitation of the angel sitting in the tomb, and of the women coming with spices to anoint the body of Jesus. When he who sits in the tomb beholds the three brethren approaching him, like lost people who are searching for something, let him sing in a sweet voice of medium pitch, "Quem quaeritis in sepulchro, O Christicolae?" (Whom seek ye in the sepulchre, O Christian women).'

These stage directions issued in the tenth century by Ethelwold, Bishop of Winchester, mark the beginning of theatre in England —a theatre which, like its Athenian predecessor, was conceived in the womb of religious ritual; the play: 'The Play of the Three Maries'; the theatre: the monastic church; the actors: the Benedictine monks; the audience: the people of England.

Once initiated, the rapid evolution of this new form of liturgy was impossible to curb. The earliest form of liturgical drama was introduced to illustrate the message of the Resurrection on one particular occasion—the Easter Mass—but it soon was used to illustrate other incidents of the New Testament. Not only did suitable enactments accompany the masses during the relevant feast days, but the Old Testament stories were drawn upon to illustrate an annual sermon on the pronouncements of the prophets. Thus the stories of *The Creation, The Fall, The Deluge, The Sacrifice of Isaac,* as well as the pronouncements of *The Prophets,* became a natural prologue to the culminating dramas of the Christian message—*Christ's Nativity, The Shepherds, the Magi, The Slaughter of the Innocents, Christ's Ministry, The Passion, The Resurrection,* and so on. Inevitably the dramatic and spectacular features of this vast, cosmic drama encroached upon the purely symbolic. And there was room for comedy, too, in the earthy characters of Noah's wife, the Shepherds, and, not least, the devils who accompanied the erring souls to hell. Costume and elements of scenery crept in, and spoken dialogue took the place of chanting. As in the development of the Athenian drama, the ritual was gradually pushed aside by the lusty demands of action, character, and spectacle. By the twelfth century, religious drama was no longer a semi-dramatic, semi-liturgical ritual, but a highly organized 'show'. The plays required many months of preparation and their cost was often considerable. This drama was not, of course, intended by the Church for the entertainment or recreation of the spectators, its purpose was to combine worship and doctrine in a form that could readily be understood by every man; and the dramatic form was equipped to do this even more powerfully than the mosaics, the paintings, and the sculpture of the great Norman and Gothic cathedrals from which it sprang. It was from this desire to reach the heart of the common man and to inspire him to a greater spiritual awakening that the vulgar tongue was introduced in the place of Latin in the plays of the early fourteenth century. Shyly at first, but soon to be universally adopted, the English-speaking drama was born. The dialogue was couched in homely rhyme which reflected the colloquialisms of everyday speech and with the introduction of native speech the action of the plays themselves became steadily more real and the characters more human.

The increasing demands made by this theatrical liturgy upon

the time of the priestly performers, the need to impersonate female characters and such undesirable persons as Judas Iscariot, the ranting Herod and the Devil himself, as well as animals, such as Balaam's ass, caused a serious interruption of monastic life. The monks were rehearsing their parts in the cloisters, dressing themselves up in unsuitable costumes, inventing ingenious bits of business, painting the scenery and, no doubt, their faces. The churches were transformed into theatres and crowded with wondering, laughing, excited spectators. The sanctuaries themselves were in danger of desecration. The whole business had got wildly out of hand; for the Christian Church, like the Dionysian worship of Athens, had given birth to a totally uncontrollable child which was clearly destined to disrupt the whole life of the household, unless it was speedily pushed out of doors. So out into the squares in front of the churches and later into the streets and market-places went the *enfant terrible*, still guided by the church—for goodness knows what pranks it might have got up to if left to its own devices—but with at least the more disreputable characters performed by those with less reputation to lose than the priests who would be hearing confession on the following day. Released from the awe-inspiring precincts of the churches, the theatre gave vent to its joyful zest for life.

'Then shall the Devil come, and three or four other devils with him, bearing in their hands chains and iron shackles, which they shall place on the necks of Adam and Eve. And certain ones shall push them and others shall drag them towards Hell. And those waiting for them as they come shall make a great dancing and jubilation over their destruction. And other devils shall, one after another, point to them as they come; and they shall take them up and thrust them into Hell. And thereupon they shall cause a great smoke to arise, and they shall shout one to another in Hell, greatly rejoicing. And they shall dash together their pots and kettles, so that they may be heard without. And after some little interval, the devils shall go forth, and shall run to and fro in the square.'

These stage directions are from the Anglo-Norman play, *Le Jeu D'Adam*, of the twelfth century.

What effect did all this dashing together of pots and pans and running to and fro in the square have upon the spectator? Did it provoke terror or mirth? Probably the latter; but, since laughter is a great debunker of vice, no great harm was done to the moral precepts of religion, though it was to be doubted if the monks themselves should continue to take part in such vulgarities to further the aims of the Church. For, once out of doors, not only did drama become more secular and theatrical, it also became influenced by the special characteristics and requirements of open-air performance. Climatic conditions made it impossible to perform the plays on the festivals they were intended to illustrate; neither Christmas nor Easter, around which most of the plays were centred, offer congenial conditions for open-air performances. The feast of Corpus Christi, however, which was associated with an open-air procession, and which occurs in late May or early June, offered a suitable opportunity to bring the whole 'corpus' of the plays together in a vast pageant of Christian teaching. These Cycles of plays took two or three days to perform, and obviously required considerable finance and organization, since outdoor performance makes great demands on pageantry and spectacle—elements previously provided by the architecture, painted interiors, stained-glass windows, and ritual of the churches themselves. The performance of the plays became influenced by other open-air forms of pageantry, such as the elaborate ritual of the tournaments and the gorgeous street pageants organized for the royal progresses through the cities. The Cycles became increasingly elaborate, requiring vast numbers of actors, costumes, and scenic contrivances. It was clear that the monasteries were not equipped to handle such a theatre and, as it was no longer desirable for them to maintain too close or too obvious a connexion with it, direct responsibility for organization was handed over to the civic authorities and more specifically to the great Trade Guilds, since these powerful and wealthy organizations possessed a highly developed sense of social and religious responsibility.

The Guild Cycles

Consequently, it was upon the mercers, the fishmongers, the grocers, the tilers, the goldsmiths, and so on that the major tasks of organizing theatrical performances devolved. Each Trade Guild, or Craft, was required to perform a particular incident in the vast pageant or the religious Cycles. Usually the scene was allotted to a Guild according to the nature of the craft itself, or to the associations of its patron saint. Thus, the Waterleaders and Dyers undertook the staging of *The Deluge*, the Tile Thatchers undertook *The Birth of Jesus*, the Glovers *The Killing of Abel*, whilst *The Harrowing of Hell* was suitably performed under the patronage of the Cooks and Innkeepers.

Whilst the trade corporations accepted responsibility for mounting and financing the great Cycles of plays, it must not be imagined that the Church severed all connexion with them. The many unbeneficed clergy—clerks and friars—were employed as authors, copyists, and pageant masters, whilst the local abbot or bishop often guided, and sometimes censored, the arrangements made by the mayors and the Guilds. The play Cycles were still regarded by the Church as important instruments of religious propaganda, though they became increasingly a highly popular form of secular entertainment. Once outside the churches, the plays were presented in different ways to suit local conditions, but no such thing as a permanent built theatre was used; except in Cornwall, where circular open-air arenas were constructed. Generally it appears that one of the following methods of presentation was employed.

The earliest form of staging in the open air was probably a direct adaptation of the method of setting out the scenes employed in the churches. By this method the scenes which were called 'mansions'—and which were clearly often elaborate structures in and around which the action of each play revolved—were set out in rectangular formation like the booths in the market-place or the sets in a TV studio. The audience moved from mansion to mansion and the plays were performed consecutively. This method continued until the end of the religious play tradition, as the sketch for the Lucerne Easter play of 1583 shows.

The more usual method of staging in England, however, was that normally adopted by the Guilds, which was to mount the mansions on wagons and draw them through the streets like tableaux vivants in a carnival procession. These mobile 'pageants', as they were called, were halted in turn at prearranged places in the town where an audience was awaiting them. Each play was then presented consecutively in the pageant cart, or on an open wagon which was drawn up in front of it and acted as a fore-stage to it. Sometimes, too, the action was extended into the street itself.

A third method was to build the mansions in a line or semi-circle with a common acting area in front of them, known as the 'platea', which was sometimes raised and sometimes the street or market square itself. This method is illustrated by the miniature of the sixteenth-century Valenciennes *Passion Play* and is still employed at Einsiedeln near Lucerne, where a religious play is annually performed.

There was, therefore, no set way of performing the plays; much depended on local conditions and traditions; but clearly the medieval play directors, *Maîtres des feintes* as they were called, were searching for a suitable form. The problems they had to solve were similar to those of the ancient Greeks and to the problems of open-air performance today. The problem of sight-lines was solved by the raised stage—the cart in the case of the processional method and the raised 'platea' in the case of the static method. Acoustics were probably often unsatisfactory, but the choice of market-places and areas surrounded by buildings was clearly an attempt to overcome this constant problem of open-air performance. The age-old problem of how to avoid long waits between scenes was solved by the procession of pageants on the one hand and by the multiple scenes served by a common stage on the other. Lastly, there was the problem of illusion.

In the earliest liturgical drama the action was largely symbolic and little illusion was required. The sepulchre was a recess in the wall beside the altar—where it is still to be seen in many early churches—and by placing the cross in it and removing the cross from it the action of Burial and Resurrection was satisfactorily represented. The costumes of the three 'Maries' were no more than the white-hooded robes of the priests and neither wigs nor make-up would have been contemplated. But once liturgy changed into play-acting the search for illusion and realism began. The 'mansions' were made to represent Heaven and Hell, the Garden of Eden, Noah's Ark, the Stable of Bethlehem, the Palace of Herod, the Upper Room for the Last Supper. The Crucifixion and the Ascension had to be contrived and built with great skill and realism. Machinery had to be introduced to provide flames, smoke, descents and ascents. Music and choirs were required; so, too, were professional dancers. Costumes had to be made; a pair of gloves and a white beard for God; masks and tails with fireworks attached for the devils; a special costume and beard for Herod; and so on. Though much of the costuming was contemporary in the style of the religious paintings of the twelfth to the sixteenth century, expenses mounted: much time had to be spent on labour and rehearsals, and bread and ale had to be purchased to feed and refresh the many actors and craftsmen. Finally, many actors had to be paid, and some had to be hired from other towns to fill the more important parts. On the Continent master carpenters and play directors were beginning to travel from place to place as their renown increased. The theatre was not only discovering its form, it was increasingly becoming a full-time profession and experiencing the financial problems that have remained its major worry and often caused its defeat.

Some idea of the size and scope of the Guild Cycles can be gained from the elaborate stage directions and the inventories of costumes and properties. The pageant-cars, too, on which the plays were performed were highly elaborate and costly vehicles; usually built in two stories, covered with fine cloth, ornamented with gilded figures, painted in bright colours, and drawn by a team of horses decked out in expensive trappings. The pageant-car of the Norwich grocers included in its inventory '6 Horses clothes, stayned, with knopps and tassels'. Today the Lord Mayor's show in London preserves something of the tradition of these decorated and elaborate 'floats'.

From our point of view the interesting feature of this growing English theatre is that it was essentially a theatre for the people; a thoroughly popular entertainment which drew huge crowds of citizens and apprentices, as well as country people from the surrounding villages, and which was spread throughout the length and breadth of the land; for the biblical cycles were not con-centrated in the capital, nor only in the larger cities. London, in fact, took very little part in the biblical plays, which were performed not only in Leicester, Wakefield, Norwich, Chester, and York, but also in small communities such as New Romney, Bungay, Braintree, Beverley, and Kingston-on-Thames. Some-thing of the richness of this early dramatic writing can be gleaned from the number of plays that are still extant—a small percent-age, however, of those that must have been written. Of the four Cycles that we still possess York has forty-two plays, Chester twenty-five, Wakefield (the Towneley Cycle) thirty-two, and Coventry forty-two. It is important, too, to remember that the older liturgical theatre, as presented by the monasteries, was a European theatre which—by reason of the universality of Catholic ritual, the contacts maintained between monastic establishments and the use of a common dramatic language—developed to a similar pattern. The Trade Guilds, however, were more removed from these continental contacts than the Church; and so the Guild Cycles developed national and, indeed, regional charac-teristics.

By the end of the fifteenth century a new spirit was abroad which was to break up the pageant cars and eventually the monasteries which had inspired them. At Bungay in 1514 certain ill-disposed persons 'brake and threw down five pageants' which were used for plays at the annual theatre festival of Corpus Christi. The spirit of Puritanism, resulting from the influence of Wycliff and the Lollards, was born, and the theatre was preparing to undergo its next great persecution at the hands of the Church. From 1500 onwards the corporations were gradually infiltrated by those who regarded theatre as a provocation to sin and a demon-stration of profanity and superstition. With the Reformation, religious plays began to assume a more sinister aspect in the eyes of the central government; for not only was much of their subject matter connected with 'popish' practices, but their great popularity ensured them large audiences. Thus they came to be regarded as dangerous and seditious political propaganda. Although in some districts the plays lingered on until 1570 and even later, they gradually fell a victim of persecution. It is, however, important to remember that, even during Shakespeare's lifetime, these plays were still being performed in some parts of England, and something of their pageantry and stagecraft influenced the form of popular English theatre until its final destruction by the Puritans under the Commonwealth.

CHAPTER SIX

A PLEA FOR PAGEANTRY

SOME PROBLEMS OF PRODUCING MEDIEVAL MYSTERY PLAYS

IT is a sad reflection on our national theatre that this heritage of vigorous pageant theatre is not more frequently performed. The plays are not great literary nor great acting dramas, nor suited to performance on a proscenium stage, but they are ideally suited to large-scale and imaginative pageant performance; offering a vast number of parts, opportunities for skilful production, and providing a worth-while community effort. As E. Martin Browne, Glynne Wickham, and others have shown, in the revivals of the York, Towneley, and Chester Cycles, they can provide these towns and cities with which they were associated with a sense of pride in their local history and culture, and at the same time act as a strong tourist attraction. A striking example of all these advantages is, of course, the Oberammergau Passion Play.

Text Editing

As in the case of Greek drama we are presented with a problem of how to convey the meaning and style of the text; for, although the plays are written in English, it is an English which is often too unfamiliar to be understood by a popular audience, and the plays are written in a regional speech the characteristics of which have largely disappeared.

The problem of editing or translating this speech is, of course, not so great as translation from another language, but the stylistic problems are more subtle. The lost regional character of the original language demands some form of equivalent dialect; for, when spoken in standard English, the jingling rhymes sound too naïve and sometimes too sanctimonious. Since the writers of regional speech are rapidly disappearing or degenerating into Mummerset linguists, the difficulty in finding a vigorous and earthy equivalent to the medieval speech is considerable. Secondly, the texts are not great works of art; for the dramatists were concerned more with their doctrinal content than with their literary or dramatic values. Repetition abounds, characterization is far from realistic and often inconsistent, dramatic points are blurred, and climax is usually ignored. There are, of course, exceptions. *The Sacrifice of Isaac* from the Broome Manor text is a satisfying play in its own right. *The Second Shepherd's Play* and *The Deluge* from the Towneley Cycle contain good characterization and can stand up to individual performance, but on the whole the plays can only impress themselves upon an audience, as they were originally designed to do, when their total impact as a Cycle has been experienced. This impact is not so much a dramatic experience as the impact of a total philosophy, the revelation of an outlook, and a way of life which we have lost. But whether presented as an entire Cycle over a period of days or whether a short section of the Cycle is performed, the plays require some skilled carpentry to join loose ends together. Again it must be pointed out that this is not a case of adaptation. The less we do to the texts the better; for nothing is more sickening than the treatment they have received from time to time by the Mrs. Grundy editors who reduce them to a language said to be suitable for performance by the Church Guild. Such versions are usually accompanied by suggestions as to how they may be performed without the sacrilegious appearance of God or Christ on the stage, which is about as sensible as a performance of *Hamlet* without the Prince.

The translator or editor should confine his task to removing the redundancies which result both from inexperienced writing and from over-emphasis on doctrinal points of no value in the theatre, and to translating the archaic regional speech into a living regional speech which can be understood by a contemporary audience.

5. Medieval Mansions.
The Valenciennes Passion Play (1547).

6. 'A platform raised upon trestles.'
The theatre of the market place.

Staging

The same editors who devote their energies to cleaning up the texts are often anxious to tell us how to stage them. Usually these instructions inform us that the plays can be performed in the church, providing the altar is decently hidden by a curtain and a light is shone on an empty chair whilst God's words are spoken off-stage. They suggest that the scenes should be properly separated by drawing a curtain between each and that the whole Cycle should be made to seem as like well-made amateur theatricals in the village hall tradition as possible.

To start with, it would be wise to recognize that these Leviathans cannot be squeezed into pint pots. We are not dealing with religious playlets, but with a huge cosmic drama which ideally should be presented in its entirety with full pageantry and spectacle. Such a performance may take several days to present, will require expert marshalling of local forces, and will entail a lot of hard work. Perhaps the best way of handling the plays would be to allot each play to a separate dramatic group, much as was originally done with the performances of the Trade Guilds, and appoint a producer-in-chief to co-ordinate the various activities. Whilst this procedure might entail more co-operation between dramatic groups than the annual festivals organized by the Drama League, it would have the advantage of a main theme and a worthier motive than mere 'pot-hunting'.

The question of staging must largely depend on locality. The interior of the church or cathedral may not be ideal to a modern audience's requirements, for, with fixed pews, the audience cannot perambulate from 'mansion' to 'mansion', and a central stage either in the aisle itself or in the chancel may present problems of sightlines. A large hall such as a college refectory or tithe-barn may be better suited to a central stage on which the 'mansions' can be arranged in the form of a multiple setting. If climatic risks are to be taken, then an open-air performance will offer greater opportunities for pageantry. But, whatever method is employed, pageantry is an essential feature of the mystery or biblical plays, and it is significant that the medieval producers of these spectacles were often referred to as the Pageant Masters and

the carts themselves referred to as Pageants. Liberal use of music
and choir, fireworks and smoke, trumpets and banners, richly
painted cloth, and gaily caparisoned horses (though perhaps not
in the church or college hall!) will help to provide the festival that
the bare texts alone scarcely suggest. And for costume let us at
all events avoid the authentic biblical garb of the children's bible.
These sickly illustrations were unknown to the medieval performers, and to a modern audience they smack of the Sunday
school. Let us have knights in armour to surround King Herod,
and let Annas and Caiaphas be dressed as Princes of the Church
and crowned with their 'myghters'. Let there be a 'camell' for
Joseph and a 'shipp' for Noah; let the three kings enter 'ridying
worshupfully with a sterr afor them'; let Pilate be accompanied
by 'his lady and his knights well beseyn', and let the Angel
Gabriel have 'a new coat and a peir of hoes'. In fact let us commit
every anachronism to recapture the teeming, vital religion that
was not part of life, but the whole of it: the leisure and work, the
arts and crafts, the vices and pleasures of the people of England.

CHAPTER SEVEN

THE PROFESSIONAL THEATRE

THE STROLLING PLAYERS AND THE PUBLIC THEATRES

MEANWHILE, a new type of theatrical entertainment had been growing up side by side with the religious Cycles. This was a compact form of entertainment, performed by professional actors, in the great halls of the nobility as well as for the entertainment of the wealthier merchants and the leaders of the Church. The origin of the professional strolling players can be traced back to the troupes of minstrels, jugglers, conjurors, dancers, and jesters banded together under the leadership of a troubadour, who performed variety entertainments to aristocratic audiences on special occasions; such occasions might be a betrothal, a marriage, the visit of an important personage, the conclusion of a day of tournament, and, of course, the Christmas and Twelfth Night festivities which have always been associated with dramatic and semi-dramatic activities, and which today stretch from charades to the annual visit to the pantomime. The professional troupes were often attached to the households of the nobility and to the royal household, though sometimes they were private companies hiring themselves out independently. Dr. Glynne Wickham has traced the influence of the elaborate ritual of the tournament as well as of other forms of medieval pageantry upon stage-craft, and the gradual emergence of the short plays, called moralities or interludes, as the main feature of the players' repertoire. The serious student of English drama is strongly advised to read his scholarly and fascinating study of this subject.[1] The plays they

[1] *Early English Stages 1300 to 1660.* Volume I: 1300 to 1576 (Routledge & Kegan Paul).

performed were at first mainly religious in character, but the conditions in which they were acted made it impossible to attempt anything so ambitious as the historical biblical plays presented in the open air by a huge crowd of amateur players financed by the wealthy Trade Guilds. New types of plays had to be devised which could be given by these small bands of itinerant actors, and the form of presentation simplified and made sufficiently flexible to meet the various conditions.

The Moralities & Interludes

Towards the end of the fifteenth century, two influences were at work which, when fused with Catholic philosophy, conditioned the type of play which evolved. On the one hand, there was the aristocratic influence of chivalry as exemplified in romance literature with its particular leaning towards allegory; on the other, there was the increasing scholastic interest in the plays of the Latin writers which provided neatly constructed plots and only required a small cast of actors and a minimum of scenery. And so there arose a new type of short play, easily performed in a great chamber or in a market square, moral in character, allegorical in treatment, and economical in construction. The characters of these 'moralities' and 'interludes', as they were called, were abstractions such as vices and virtues surrounding a central character representing mankind. This type of drama, though it might be dogmatic in content, was far more flexible than the historical plays of the Bible, and consequently better able to adapt itself to meet the changes necessitated by political and religious pressure. It could, indeed it did, become a purely secular and human drama, divorced from religious purpose. *Everyman*, an English adaptation of a Dutch play, is far more human than the abstract names of its characters suggest. Death meets Everyman, who is wasting his time in the company of Good Fellowship, Kindred, Cousin, and Goods, and warns him of his fate. Everyman begs each of his companions to accompany him on his journey to death; by each he is refused; in despair he turns to Good Deeds and Knowledge who lead him safely to the grave and the prospect of redemption. In these new plays, which were divorced from the historical situations and characters of the Bible, the writers were able to make greater use of their imaginative and creative powers. Contemporary life peeped through the abstract names, and colloquialisms were interspersed with the jingling rhymes.

Side by side with these moral plays, the vaudeville origin of the players' repertoire persisted in jigs which were sometimes elaborated into semi-literary, semi-improvised drama, in which dancing and singing were mingled with spoken dialogue in such crude entertainments as the various Sword Plays, Morris Dances, and Robin Hood plays.

With their carts containing the simple requirements of their trade, the descendants of Thespis of Icaria wandered off in search of an audience and a living. The plots of the interludes and moralities were somewhat repetitive, as their titles indicate—*Everyman, Mankind, Wyt and Science, The Interlude of Youth*—but, since the players only visited at rare intervals, this lack of variety was not too noticeable. As reformist zeal spread during the course of the sixteenth century the profession of play-acting became increasingly hazardous, and without the protection of some great lord, whose anger the puritanical aldermen did not dare to arouse, the independent companies were hounded and whipped from place to place until eventually they could scarcely find a place to lay their heads. Even such protected companies as the King's Players, the Lord Chamberlain's, the Marquis of Exeter's and others mentioned in Thomas Cromwell's account books of 1530 found a livelihood in the provinces hard to come by, for the citizens of the large provincial cities, which had previously housed the great Guild Cycles, were coming more and more under the Puritan influence. The dissolution of the monasteries and the end of the feudal system deprived the countryside of much of its local culture and individual outlook. Wealth and learning became concentrated in London and the university towns of Oxford and Cambridge. As wealthy and educated society began to form round the universities and the Court, and as the landlords left their estates to reside, at least for part of the year, in the capital, so the strolling players too began to look to London for their major source of income.

The Renaissance Plays

A new type of play was required to meet the taste of the metropolitan audience. The destruction of the great monastic schools inculcated a more general knowledge of Roman history and secular literature, and Latin plays were performed in the schools and universities as an exercise in rhetoric and grammar. This new learning was reflected in the plays. The old moralities and interludes, which were impregnated with Catholic philosophy, gave way to rough and ready imitations of Plautus, Terence, and Seneca. But throughout the greater part of the sixteenth century society was split into factions, and into widely different levels of education. The old religion clung on in the country districts; Puritanism flourished in the cities; Latin plays were performed in the universities and in the Inns of Court, and adapted translations of them were beginning to be favoured by the Court itself. The return to Catholicism during the reign of Mary added to the confusion and helped to prolong the life of Catholic drama. To please these diverse societies and changeable tastes, the players extended their repertoire to include a number of different styles of plays, or wrote and patched together plays which contained elements acceptable to all. Thus there grew up a large variety of secular play texts of very unequal merit, some little more than improvisations, intended to please the different audiences from which the players earned their living. For the nobility there were interludes as well as romantic comedies with a classical slant, such as Medwell's *Fulgens and Lucrece* and tragi-comedies like Thomas Preston's *Cambises*, which Sir Philip Sidney described as 'neither right tragedy, nor right comedy, mingling kings and clowns'. For the lawyers and the scholars there were tragedies adapted from Seneca, such as the enormously tedious *Gorboduc* by Thomas Norton and Thomas Sackville, and comedies in the manner of Plautus and Terence such as *Gammer Gurton's Needle*, by Mr. S., Master of Arts, and the boisterous *Ralph Roister Doister* by Nicholas Udal, the headmaster of Eton and Winchester. For the populace there were folk plays such as *Robin Hood and the Friar*. The players who visited Claudius' Court in *Hamlet* are aptly described by Polonius as—

The best actors in the world, either for tragedy, comedy, history, pastoral, pastoral-comical, historical-pastoral, tragical-historical, tragical-comical-historical-pastoral, scene indivisable, or poem unlimited: Seneca cannot be too heavy, nor Plautus too light for the law of writ, and the liberty: these are the only men.

This description reflects something of the confused repertoire of the strolling players whom Shakespeare must have often seen in his youth.

The staging of such plays was necessarily often simplified to the bare essentials—a platform raised upon trestles served as a stage, backed by a curtained booth which acted as dressing-room or 'tiring-house' and at the same time provided a background to the action from which entrances were made on to the stage. Since the booth was unroofed, a ladder placed inside it allowed players to appear over the top—a device that served as a rough form of balcony or upper window. Such were the bare essentials of the craft—substantially the same as those used by the old Atellan mimes. But for special occasions, when performing at Court or at a nobleman's feast, the strolling players were able to mount their plays more elaborately, and no doubt they made use of the scenic constructions employed in the 'disguisings' or 'mummings' of the aristocracy. In general it can be said that amateur performance was far more spectacular than the plays of the professionals. In the universities, schools, Inns of Court, and in the great households considerable care was lavished on the construction of scenic elements for a play. For the disguisings and mummings, which were arranged for special occasions, castles, mountains, arbours, grottos, and ships transformed the hall or the chamber into a fairyland of allegorical objects. No less elaborate and costly were the great street pageants and processions with their ornamental, symbolic arches, which welcomed the sovereign during the royal progresses through the provinces or on his return to his capital. In comparison with such costly spectacles the strolling players were poorly provided; but the players would often take part in these semi-dramatic activities, performing a jig at a masque, mouthing a thunderous speech of welcome from a decorated triumphal arch, or acting a part in a religious Cycle at

Corpus Christi. From all these dramatic and semi-dramatic events they collected ideas which were to enrich the pageantry of their own stage when eventually they came to possess a home of their own.

The Professional Theatres

One day perhaps a troupe of strolling players with their cart wandered into an inn in London where they brought good custom to the landlord and were invited to stay on until they became a regular feature of the house. Their cart with its booth provided stage and 'tiring' house, whilst the balconies of the inn courtyard were admirably suited to the accommodation of the audience. And so James Burbage conceived the idea of a permanent London playhouse in 1576, and, following the pattern of the cart in the open yard surrounded by balconies, he built The Theatre. His example was speedily followed, and soon a number of open-air, or 'public' theatres, were erected around the capital—the Curtain, the Rose, the Swan, the Globe, the Fortune were all built between 1577 and 1600. The players dared not brave the anger of the aldermen by building their theatres inside the city itself, but London covered a comparatively small area, and the jurisdiction of the aldermen did not stretch to the south bank of the Thames nor to Finsbury Fields, in which areas the 'public' playhouses were built. The old problems of the professional players were at an end once permanent homes had been established, but new problems arose. The audience, now brought together in one place, could no longer be treated as separate entities of scholars, lawyers, citizens, nobles, and countrymen, for the theatres were frequented by all types at once, with a liberal sprinkling of prostitutes, cut-purses, and confidence-men drawn thither by the opportunities of trade. Plays were no longer a rarity which only appeared, like the circus, once or twice a year; to earn their living the actors had to draw an audience every day. The days of the amateur dramatists were ended. Plays were required in great numbers to fill out the repertoire. Professional writers were hired by the resident companies to meet the enormous demand for new plays, and as the same audience came more and more frequently to the playhouses, so the playgoers grew more and more critical of the standards of playwriting and acting. Education, too, was becoming more general and its standards were rising in the new grammar schools. Out of the old and new learning new plays had to be written. From the mixture of tragedy and comedy, with its liberal use of violence and bloodshed of which Sidney complained in *Cambises,* from the pageantry and spectacle of the religious plays and from the moralities and interludes arose Christopher Marlowe; the first significant poet-dramatist of the British stage. *Tamburlaine,* with its great and thundering speech, its spirit of adventure, its sense of the vastness and greatness of human enterprise unaided by divine intervention, fitted the growing self-confidence of Renaissance society.

Marlowe and the Elizabethans

During the brief period of six years, from 1587, when *Tamburlaine Part One* probably first appeared with Edward Alleyn in the leading part, until the playwright's death in a tavern brawl in 1593, Marlowe almost succeeded in transforming the English play from a folk play into a theatrical work of art. Had he lived longer he might well have become the Aeschylus to Shakespeare's Sophocles and provided a mighty rival to his successor.

In the opening lines of *Tamburlaine Part One* Marlowe proudly announced his intention of raising the art of playwriting from folk mumming to high tragedy in the Greek sense.

> From jigging veins of rhyming mother wits,
> And such conceits as clownage keeps in pay,
> We'll lead you to the stately tents of war,
> Where you shall hear the Scythian Tamburlaine
> Threatening the world with high astounding terms,
> And scourging kingdoms with his conquering sword. . . .

Unfortunately his death at the age of thirty deprived the English stage of the full development of his dramatic powers. Of his five plays, *Tamburlaine* (c. 1587), *The Tragical History of Doctor Faustus* (1588), *The Jew of Malta* (c. 1589), *Edward II,* and *Dido, Queen of Carthage* (c. 1593), probably his play on the Faust legend was his greatest achievement. Unfortunately, the play was not published during his lifetime; it was subsequently altered and new scenes interpolated by later actor-dramatists anxious to exploit the popular taste for low comedy, but from the scenes which are pure Marlowe we can judge of the playwright's power. The last scene where Faustus, alone in his study, waits for the striking of the clock which is to bring him to death and damnation is among the most effective dramatic scenes ever written:

> The stars move still, time runs, the clock will strike,
> The devil will come, and Faustus must be damned.
> O, I'll leap up to my God!—Who pulls me down?—
> See, see, where Christ's blood streams in the firmament!
> One drop would save my soul, half a drop:
> Ah, my Christ!—

With *Faustus* came for the first time in English playwriting the effective growth of character. This, beside the introduction of truly poetic speech, is perhaps Marlowe's greatest contribution to our theatre. Between the first act and the last Faustus develops as a man, moving from self-sufficiency to despair. Marlowe freed the stage of its dependence on didactic legend and outworn ritual and allowed it to breathe new life in the imaginative world of the aspiring Renaissance mind.

With Marlowe came other professional playwrights. In 1589 Thomas Kyd wrote one of the most popular plays of the age, *The Spanish Tragedy*, in which he adopted the full-blooded drama of Seneca with its murders, its ghosts, and its madness, and so gave birth to the popular plays of revenge, which enjoyed the same sort of vogue as detective plays in our own century. John Lyly (1554–1606) introduced prose into comedy. His plays, often written as pastorals with an arcadian background, brought elegance and contemporary satire to the stage. *Endimion, the Man in the Moon* and *Campaspe* were written for performance by the Children of St. Paul's and of the Chapel Royal, new and dangerous rivals to the professional companies, later to be satirized by Shakespeare as 'an aery of children, little eyases that cry out on the top of question, and are most tyrannically clapped for't'; George Peele with his 'pleasant, conceited comedie', *The Old Wives Tale* (*c.* 1590), found a popular mixture of romance and folk comedy: Thomas Dekker (*c.* 1572–1632) appealed to the good citizens of London in *The Shoemaker's Holiday*: Robert Greene with his *History of Friar Bacon and Friar Bungay* (*c.* 1589) mingled the court and the country people in a poetic and romantic love story. All these and many other dramatists were weaving and spinning the infinite variety of Elizabethan drama, sometimes working singly, sometimes combining together as in *The Witch of Edmonton* (Dekker and Middleton) to satisfy the professional companies with their huge demand for plays—plays which contained all the elements required by the mixed audiences and plays that would please the increasingly high critical standards which resulted from the habit of regular theatregoing. From 1576, when Burbage's Theatre was established, until the end of the century, the professional English theatre grew up from childhood to maturity at a rate unprecedented in dramatic history. It was inevitable that its full flowering would result in a genius of no common kind. And so the stage was set for the glory that was Shakespeare.

Shakespeare—the Professional

Like most of the world's great men, Shakespeare arrived at a moment in time when conditions were most favourable to the gifts he had to offer. The stage on which he was to work provided a skilled craftsman with unprecedented opportunities of earning a living. Even if the players were unfavourably regarded by the civic authorities, they were beloved by the majority of the citizens, protected by the aristocracy, and smiled upon by the court. In such a profession it was possible for the humble son of a Stratford glover to mix with the university wits and with the bejewelled noblemen who delighted as much in trying their hand at turning a sonnet or writing a play as they did in working their hounds or handling their rapiers. Stable government and civil justice encouraged the cultivation of leisure, and this in turn gave rise to healthy competition between theatres to gain the public's favour and to rising standards of entertainment. For the first time in English theatrical history two 'star' actors arose whose names became household words—Richard Burbage of the Theatre and later of the Globe, and Edward Alleyn of the Rose and later of the Fortune; while at the Blackfriars the children of the Chapel Royal and St. Paul's competed strongly for popular favour.

The city itself offered a mine of inspiration to the young man from Warwickshire with a quick eye to observe its characters and a ready ear to catch their modes of speech. London was a small city and still closely in touch with the rural life of the country. In the fields of Piccadilly a botanist might cull wild flowers and in the marshes of Islington the wild-fowler might find good sport. The river had become the market-place for world trade and the gateway to adventure; down its broad stream came foreigners with strange manners and travellers with wondrous tales. The dark days of religious and feudal strife were over; a new spirit of nationhood was born and freedom of thought and expression was breaking through the old prejudices and taboos. But London still provided its darker amusements to draw the crowds away from the playhouses. The cruelties of the bear-pit, the 'rascal beadle' at the whipping post, the gruesome dramas at Tyburn, and the decaying heads on Tower Bridge—these found their grim counterpart in the plays of the period side by side with the sweets of poetry and music. In this 'quick forge' a young man from Stratford found 'infinite riches in a little room'.

Between 1587 (the date is uncertain) and 1613 Shakespeare wrote some thirty-odd plays and collaborated in the writing of others. Some have doubted if such a prodigious output could have been the work of a man who was also an actor, a successful dealer in property, a theatre shareholder, as well as a writer of one hundred and fifty-four sonnets and several major poems. The anti-Stratfordians have put forward the claims of men of wider experience and greater education. The name of Sir Francis Bacon, the Earl of Oxford, the Earl of Derby, Sir Edward Dyer have been advanced with much heated argument and even Christopher Marlowe has been resurrected from his early grave to bear the immortal pen. Yet none of these in their writings displayed the characteristics of the professional hand that wrote the plays. It is a hand that is unmistakable to all who act or produce his plays—a hand that Ivor Brown has rightly called 'the hand of glory'.[1] Others have sought to provide Shakespeare with the experience and education which they felt could hardly have been acquired by a common player educated at a country grammar school. And during the years before he emerged as a major poet and playwright he has been credited with serving as a sailor, a schoolmaster, a private tutor, a lawyer, and a sergeant in the army. Literary detectives have searched the records and sifted the legends that have grown around his personality to discover what sort of man he was, but the man stands clearly enough before us in the sweetness, elevation of spirit, indignation, despair, and in the final calm of his plays, but above all in his dedication to his profession.

[1] *Shakespeare*, Collins, 1949.

CHAPTER EIGHT

POETIC ACTION

SHAKESPEARE'S STAGE-CRAFT AND CONTEMPORARY PRODUCTION

ENOUGH has been written about Shakespeare's plays to fill a library. There can be no point in summarizing what has been said better elsewhere. But now that we have reached a point, in our survey of the theatre, when actors and playwrights could settle down to the serious business of developing their craft, it might be suitable if we paused to consider what was the stagecraft of the Elizabethan theatre. However we may choose to produce Shakespeare's plays today, we cannot afford to overlook the conditions which governed their construction—namely, the stage itself and the style of acting practised upon it.

'It was the happiness of the actors of those times,' wrote Richard Flecknoe in his memories of Burbage, 'to have such poets as these to instruct them, and write for them; and no less of those poets to have such docile and excellent actors to act their plays as a Field and Burbage; of whom we may say he was a delightful Proteus, so wholly transforming himself into his part, and putting off himself with his clothes, as he never (not so much as in the Tyring-house) assumed himself again until the play was done: there being as much difference between him and one of our common actors, as between a ballad-singer who only mouths it, and an excellent singer, who knows all the graces, and can artfully vary and modulate his voice, even to know how much breath he is to give to every syllable. He had all the parts of an excellent orator (animating his words with speaking and speech with action), his auditors being never more delighted than when he spoke, nor more sorry than when he held his peace; yet even then, he was an excellent actor still, never falling in his part when he had done speaking: but with his looks and gesture, maintaining it still unto the height.'

The question of whether Elizabethan acting was formal and stylized in the classical manner, or realistic in the manner of our contemporary stage, is still a matter for debate. It would seem there were two styles in vogue: the rhetorical style favoured by Edward Alleyn who was associated with Marlowe's plays—this style was no doubt also employed by the 'little eyases' of St. Paul's whose classical education included the practice of rhetoric and oratory—and the more realistic style favoured by Richard Burbage, who was associated with most of Shakespeare's plays. The difference between the construction of the verse in Shakespeare's plays written for Burbage and that of Marlowe is strongly indicative of these two types of acting. Marlowe's mighty lines were written to be spoken with a fine rolling delivery and large sweeping gestures:

> And ride in triumph through Persepolis!
> Is it not brave to be a king, Techelles?
> Usumcasane and Theridamas,
> Is it not passing brave to be a king,
> And ride in triumph through Persepolis?

In our contemporary theatre, where realistic speech is cultivated and the art of verse-speaking in the rhetorical manner is largely frowned upon, it is hard to find actors able to undertake the major roles in Marlowe's plays; for this reason, perhaps, they are seldom performed. Actors reared on the realism of radio and television acting are often unable to adapt their technique to the style of acting that rhetorical plays require.

Shakespeare's early plays—*Henry VI Part I* and *Titus Andronicus*—were written for Lord Strange's company of which Alleyn was a member. In these early works his verse is far more rhetorical than in the plays written for Burbage. But apart from the verse, Shakespeare frequently employs prose, and prose which could not be mouthed or declaimed. Such dialogue as the following is

purely realistic and could have been written by any contemporary
dramatist.

Bernardo: Who's there?
Francisco: Nay, answer me. Stand and unfold yourself.
Bernardo: Long live the King.
Francisco: Bernardo?
Bernardo: He.
Francisco: You come most carefully upon your hour.

Ben Jonson in his comedies, also written for Burbage's
company, introduced a stage language which was almost completely colloquial and realistic; consequently Jonson's plays are
not easily understood by our contemporary audiences and,
perhaps for this reason, less frequently performed than those of
Shakespeare, Webster, and other late Elizabethans who stood at
the crossroads of realism and stylized acting. We have further
evidence of this change in style of acting in Hamlet's advice to
the players:

Hamlet: O, there be players that I have seen play, and heard others
             praise, and that highly, not to speak it profanely, that,
             neither having the accent of Christians, nor the gait of a
             Christian, pagan, nor man, have so strutted and bellowed
             that I have thought some of Nature's journeymen had
             made men and not made them well, they imitated
             humanity so abominably.
1st Player: I hope we have reform'd that indifferently with us, sir.
Hamlet: O, reform it altogether.

It is significant that this controversy between the use of realistic
and rhetorical speech in Shakespeare's plays is still raging today.
And there are few of our leading Shakespearian players who do
not incur the censure of the critics for failing to bring out the
poetry of the lines, and yet Hamlet specifically instructs his actors
in the method of speech they are to employ:

Speak the speech, I pray you, as I pronounced it to you, trippingly on
the tongue; but if you mouth it, as many of your players do, I had as
lief the town-crier spoke my lines.

The question that modern actors of Shakespeare have to answer in what does 'trippingly' mean. The answer is not to treat the verse as prose, but to give equal value to scansion and meaning. The actors of the old melodramatic school understood what scansion meant, whereas many of our younger actors have never been trained to respect the scansion of the iambic-pentameter line. The old actors may have often neglected the meaning of a line, whereas the modern actor inclines to place too heavy an emphasis on a word or a phrase in order to underline its meaning. The word 'trippingly' implies speaking in a light musical or dance measure; this is very different from 'mouthing' which implies speaking with a bombastic delivery, and different, too, from the muttering, halting delivery of realistic speech. The poetry of Shakespeare must be made to dance along and emphasis must take its place in the rhythmic flow of the line without interrupting it. There is no greater master of the Shakespearian style than John Gielgud, who has inherited from the past the understanding of scansion and has allied it to the present appreciation of meaning.

The question of speech is, of course, closely allied to that of characterization. Interpretation of character in the modern naturalistic sense means the complete identification of character and speech. If the character is completely naturalistic—drawn from life—then clearly his speech must be equally natural to that character. Thus, in interpreting the part of Firs in *The Cherry Orchard*, the actor searches for a form of speech which is in complete harmony with the character. Now, it is clear that when a character is larger than life, like Tamburlaine, his speech must be larger than life. The means by which the actor interprets the larger-than-life character of Tamburlaine will be clearly different from the means by which he interprets the character of Firs, but in both cases the object of fitting speech to the conception of character, whether the speech itself be rhetorical or naturalistic, must be consistent. In Shakespeare we are presented with a far more complex problem, for his characters use both colloquial and poetical speech often in the course of one scene. The actor of Shakespeare's plays has, therefore, to find a way of bridging the gap between poetic and common reality. He must be able to show us Hamlet as a natural man, Hamlet as he exists in his public

F

existence and Hamlet as he exists in his private existence, the higher man and the common clay. Reason and imagination have to be combined in speech and characterization at the same time, and the result must be harmonious—must be perfectly consistent —if the result is to be a work of theatrical art.

Shakespeare did not always plumb the depths of character, but he certainly drew lively pictures of human beings, especially in his low comedy types. Falstaff, Pistol, Nym, Bardolph, Dogberry and Verges, Bottom and Quince, Sir Toby Belch and Sir Andrew Aguecheek, all have an existence beyond the actual confines of their stage existence. We know how they would behave if we were to introduce them to a garden party at Buckingham Palace, or lead them into our local pub. But the noble or serious characters in Shakespeare do not lend themselves to the type of analysis that Stanislavsky used. Iago, for instance, is a villain and no deep study of motive will help to make his villainy any more effective. Just as Shakespeare's style of writing is a mixture of poetry and prose, of poetic and common speech, so his characters are both poetic and real. His genius consists in blending the two together and often his greatest effects are achieved when the two styles meet: the meeting of common reality with poetic reality in the Grave-yard scene in *Hamlet*, the dialogue between Bottom and Titania, or between the Fool and Lear.

It is to be presumed that this mixture of styles new and old was the new style of Burbage and his company. The result was a style which combined realism and poetry, and this style of Burbage and the Lord Chamberlain's men contrasted strongly with the rhetorical style of Edward Alleyn and the Lord Admiral's men. The players in *Hamlet*, despite the Prince's admonitions, are clearly playing in the latter convention, and Hamlet's reactions to their heavy melodramatic style must have been much like Shakespeare's to the style of Alleyn.

Begin, murderer, pox, leave thy damnable faces, and begin . . .

But when we talk of realism in Shakespeare we must not confuse this word with naturalistic realism, nor with psychological realism, as we understand those methods of approach to acting today. The plays of Shakespeare and his contemporaries are poetic realism and are not, as some contemporary actors and directors try to make them, primarily psychological studies of character nor minutely observed portrayals of behaviour. They are epic or story plays in which the action always comes first. The action of the play unfolds the character. It is the action of the play that makes Hamlet waver in his purpose, not because he has any compunction about killing people. Similarly it is the action which turns the gay and heartless Richard II into the sad and noble prisoner of Pomfret, which turns the proud intolerant Lear into a madman, Macbeth into a murderer and the madcap Hal into a patriot king. In other words, whilst each character has in him the seeds of change and 'one man in his time plays many parts', it is circumstances which decide which part he is to play.

The directors and actors of the plays must study and understand the story of the play—not the story as we would like to conceive it to suit our modern taste, nor the story, in an historical play, as our modern history books tell it—but the story as it was understood and felt by its author. This story must be told on the stage clearly, emphatically, dramatically, and swiftly; from it character must emerge—just as much character as is needed and no more.

No less controversial is the problem of visual presentation: the sort of theatre we require for Elizabethan drama and the sort of settings we should employ. The architecture of the 'public' theatres during Shakespeare's lifetime has become a lively source of detective literature in which theatre scholars have bandied about their ideas founded upon the most illusive direct evidence and some ingeniously constructed circumstantial evidence. The only visual evidence of the interior of a 'public' theatre of the period depends exclusively upon a rough sketch of the Swan theatre copied by Arend Van Buchell of Utrecht from an original drawing by John de Witt, which accompanied the latter's observations of the London theatres during a visit in 1596. Additional evidence can be gleaned from maps and perspective views of London, which provide some indication of the exterior appearance of the theatres, from building contracts and from observations by visitors. Finally, there is the internal evidence which can be found in the texts of the plays themselves. These sources are, however, insufficient to provide a complete or certain answer to the problem of the original staging and, in fact, have given rise to widely different views of interpretation. Until recently it was held that the stage was a bare platform projecting into the open yard of the auditorium and covered with a roof, having at the back a long balcony in which upper scenes were played, such as Juliet's balcony or the Walls of Amiens in *King John*. Under this balcony it was presumed that there was a recess in which interior scenes were played, such as the tomb of the Capulets and the bedchamber of the dying John of Gaunt. Dr. Leslie Hotson in his book *Shakespeare's Wooden O*[1] has effectively shown that the stage was, in fact, surrounded by the audience, the upper gallery contained boxes which housed the noblest patrons, and the fashionable patrons of the playhouse had stools on the stage itself immediately below these boxes. He has therefore argued that there was no under gallery, but merely a wall, as shown in the crude drawing of the Swan. His conclusions are that the Elizabethan playhouse was theatre-in-the-round.

He has further advanced the theory that two constructions, or stage houses, with curtained upper and lower stories flanked the platform stage. These were, he believes, constructed in the manner of the old pageant carts and were used for the balconies, upper rooms, and interiors in the plays.

Anyone who has had to deal with a production on an Elizabethan stage based on the assumption of balcony and under-balcony, such as exists at the Maddermarket Theatre in Norwich, will agree with Dr. Hotson that it is unsatisfactory to play an intimate scene, such as the tomb scene in *Romeo and Juliet* on the inner stage under the balcony with the whole depth of the platform between the actors and the audience. It would be even more unsatisfactory if the patrons of the highest priced seats were seated in the balcony immediately above this inner stage.

But the solution put forward by Hotson that the action of these inner and upper scenes took place inside two flanking

[1] Hart-Davis, 1960.

stage-houses and was revealed by masked mutes who drew aside the curtains presents a number of practical problems. How did the actors enter these isolated houses without being seen? And how did they get such furniture as thrones, tombs, and beds into them without carrying these through the audience or wending their way through the actors on the stage? Hotson suggests that entry to these houses was through trapdoors in the stage floor and up ladders which led from under the stage to the stage level and from the stage level to the upper stories. It may be possible to ascend a ladder in a farthingale, but to descend one is quite another matter. Nor would the mutes, who presumably man-handled Juliet's tomb and other cumbersome properties up these ladders, have remained so mute in the performance of it. That there were trapdoors in the platform stage is clear, but their use was surely for comparatively simple operations, such as raising and lowering the cauldron and apparitions in *Macbeth*.

The second problem of the stage-houses is the drawing of the curtains. Hotson suggests that both the upper and lower stories of these constructions were curtained all round. Since the audience sat all round the stage, it would be necessary for the mutes to draw all the curtains to reveal or conceal the scenes presented within them. Moreover, since there was, Hotson maintains, more than one room both on the stage level and in the upper stories, it would be necessary to draw all the curtains of all the rooms to allow everyone to see inside any single room.

Thirdly, we have the problem of the sight-lines. The patrons in the upper balcony at the rear of the stage would gain nothing, since they could not see through the floors of the upper stories of the stage-houses any more than they could see what was happening underneath them in the old assumption of acting the scenes in the inner stage, but the sight-lines from all parts of the playhouse would be impeded by these constructions. However, it is not to be concluded that Hotson is wrong—though it is hard to accept the ladders—but, if he is right, it is more likely that such stage-houses were temporary constructions which were put up only when required, and consisted only of such sections as the action of the play demanded. It would seem more likely that these constructions, when used, were set against the stage wall, where the Swan sketch shows two large doors, from which there would be access to them for the actors and property men.

C. Walter Hodges has put forward a solution to the staging of *Antony and Cleopatra* in his book *The Globe Restored*[1] which seems to me to have much merit from a production point of view. In this play, as well as in others of the period, there is an absolute requirement of an upper stage (the monument of *Antony and Cleopatra*) in which the actors must be clearly visible and, indeed, in fairly close proximity to the whole audience. It is inconceivable that the action was intended to take place in a box fronted with a balcony railing in the centre of the upper gallery. Hodges, therefore, suggests that there was a temporary upper stage, jutting out on to the stage between the two main doors of the 'tiring-house'. A similar arrangement—again of a temporary nature—could have been used to serve as the cell of Friar Lawrence and the tomb of Juliet; this time, using the lower part of the structure, whilst Juliet's balcony was above it. Such temporary structures built for particular plays would have been entirely in keeping with the medieval tradition of 'mansions'. This suggestion does not invalidate the theory that the upper balcony and the recess under the balcony were also used as acting areas on other occasions. Nor is there any reason to suppose that windows were not occasionally inserted into the upper balcony when the action called for them. On such occasions, it may be that the patrons who used the upper galleries were seated elsewhere. Today we occasionally oust the patrons to use the stage-boxes as part of our acting area or for placing our spotlights. The Swan drawing shows no recess under the balcony; this may have been because the arras was drawn across it when de Witt who witnessed a performance in the theatre was present—the drawing is, after all, remarkably crude—or because there was no under-balcony at the Swan. It would be as ludicrous to suggest that all Elizabethan playhouses had similar stages as for future historians of the twentieth century theatre to suggest that all our theatres had revolving stages or were constructed like the Mermaid. The

[1] Ernest Benn, 1953.

Fortune was rectangular; other 'public' theatres were either round or polygonal; the Hope (built in 1613) had a removable stage to enable the playhouse to be used for bear-baitings. Besides the 'public' theatres there were indoor 'private' theatres such as Blackfriars, the Cockpit, Whitefriars, and Paul's. Performances were given at Court, and on tour in the provinces, as well as overseas in Denmark and the Low Countries. It is, therefore, pointless to pursue too far all the details of stage construction in the hope that we can recapture Shakespeare's stage-craft. But it is important that we recapture the style—or general feeling—of the stage for which he wrote.

Whatever the construction of the various forms of playhouses may have been, it is clear that the stage itself was an unlocalized area, which did not attempt to present illusionary scenery, and that this convention did influence the form in which the plays were written. Atmosphere and mood, which today we build up with scenery and lighting, were in Shakespeare's day provided by the use of poetry and imagery. If, therefore, too much visual imagery is added to verbal imagery, we are in danger of destroying the effect of the latter.

When Macbeth says:

> Light thickens,
> And the crow makes wing to the rooky wood,

we may in our modern theatre benefit from the dimming of the lights, but we do not require to see the crow or the wood.

Even less in keeping with the style of Shakespeare is the effect of breaking the plays up into separate scenes. The merit of the unlocalized stage was that it allowed continuity of action, so that the whole play was seen as a continuous action. This is the same effect as the cinema is able to achieve today. A great deal of the mounting tensions as well as the contrasts of action are lost by the process of dividing the scenes between the forestage and the full stage, or by dropping the curtain between the scenes and filling out the pauses with extracts of recorded music. Poetry is expressed in movement as well as in words. The flow of Shakespeare's action must match the movement of his poetry.

CHAPTER NINE

THE THEATRE OF ILLUSION

THE INDOOR PLAYHOUSES AND
THE RESTORATION THEATRE

In 1597 Shakespeare's company acquired the roofed-in building of the Blackfriars which required some form of artificial lighting and probably greater attention to scenic illusion than was possible in the open-air theatres. It also had the effect of limiting the size and character of the audience, for the prices of admission were higher. In this atmosphere of greater intimacy the drama began to reflect the tastes of a society which was becoming increasingly class-conscious. *The Knight of the Burning Pestle* by Francis Beaumont pokes open fun at the tastes of the citizen and his wife who were the main patrons of the popular theatres. The excitement engendered by the birth of national consciousness which called forth the imaginative response of Elizabethan audiences began to degenerate into the cult of sensationalism occasionally lit by flashes of poetry. Greater stimulus was required to evoke the imagination of the more sophisticated audiences of the indoor theatres. Dark and unnatural crimes were favoured in such plays as John Ford's '*Tis Pity She's a Whore*; *A New Way to Pay Old Debts*, by Philip Massinger; *The White Devil* and *The Duchess of Malfi* by John Webster; *The Changeling* by Thomas Middleton, and *A Woman Killed with Kindness* by Thomas Heywood; whilst the bloody tragedies of Cyril Tourneur provided stimulus in plays of revenge, rape, incest, fratricide, adultery, murder, and madness. Even a domestic murder thriller was supplied in *Arden of Feversham* of uncertain authorship. Against this stream of sensation and crime, which emphasized plot rather than character, Ben Jonson strove to battle for classical reason.

The justice that the contemporary English theatre has rendered to Shakespeare carries with it an injustice to his contemporaries, and to no one more than to his close friend, Ben Jonson. Alone amongst the contemporaries of Shakespeare, Jonson stands out as a giant of almost equal stature to his friend. The fact that his plays are not frequently performed today is partly due to our own failure to establish a national playhouse where we can learn to appreciate different styles of theatre as we can and do learn to appreciate different styles of painting and music through our established institutions, and partly, to Jonson's accurate reproduction of the topical and living speech of his own day. In character he was a true Elizabethan: poet, dramatist, actor, courtier, wit, a great quarreller—he was twice imprisoned—a staunch friend and a prodigious drinker. Tradition relates that it was as a result of a drinking bout with Jonson that Shakespeare died when Jonson visited his old friend during his retirement at Stratford.

His most productive period was during the ten years from 1606 to 1616—from *Volpone* to *The Alchemist*. Like Aristophanes he delighted in an earthy obscenity; like Menander, Plautus, and Terence, he satirized greed, middle-class stupidity, credulity, and above all the narrow-minded Puritanism which threatened to destroy the theatre. In *The Alchemist, Volpone, Everyman in His Humour, The Silent Woman,* and *Bartholomew Fair,* Jonson developed the pattern of the comedy of manners.

Meanwhile in the court itself a development was taking place which was to revolutionize English stage-craft. Amateur theatricals had, as we have seen, always been a popular pastime in the great households since the early days of chivalry. Now this practice found new encouragement from James I and his queen, Anne of Denmark, who delighted in taking part in these entertainments. In the hands of Ben Jonson and the scenic artist, Inigo Jones, the old 'disguisings', now called 'masques', became even more spectacular and theatrical, combining scenery, lighting, poetry, dancing, and music. Like the old 'disguisings' the masques were usually allegorical in subject—*The Masques of Blackness and of Beauty, The Masque of Queens, Love Freed from Ignorance and Folly, Pleasure Reconciled to Virtue.* Such entertainments were even more elaborately mounted at the Italian and French courts, and from them sprang opera and ballet.

Whilst the new emphasis on scenery and lighting could have little influence on the popular open-air theatres, it could affect the 'private' theatres and in due course it was to change the whole character of the English theatre when its traditions were finally swept away by the Civil War and a new indoor theatre was born under Charles II. Amongst others who contributed to these entertainments Sir William Davenant is to be remembered, since it was he who was to bridge the chasm of oblivion into which the theatre was now to fall.

Since the suppression of the religious Cycles opposition to the professional theatre from Puritan sources had been mounting. As early as 1572 a law was passed ordering all stage companies, not under Royal or noble patronage, to be disbanded and branding the actors as 'rogues, vagabonds, and sturdy beggars'. In 1577 John Northbrook voiced the Puritan view in his *Treatise against Dicing, Dancing, Plays and Interludes, with other idle Pastimes*:

I am persuaded that Satan hath not a more speedie way and fitter schoole to work and teach his desire, to bring men and women into the snare of concupiscence and filthy lustes of wicked whoredome, than those places and plays and theatres are: and therefore necessaire that those places and players should be forbidden, and dissolved, and put down by authoritie, as the brothell houses and stewes are.

In 1597 the Lord Mayor and Aldermen of London had petitioned the Privy Council to have the theatres closed, and in every case of plague or riot the theatres were held to be the cause. In 1634 William Prynne, whilst attacking the public stage in his publication of *Histriomastix*, was unwise enough to criticize the Court masques and no less a person than Charles I's queen, Henrietta Maria, for performing in them; his ears were chopped off and he was cast into prison. In addition to the pulpit, the main strongholds of Puritan opposition were the city and town councils, and it was here that the real danger lay to the existence of the theatre, since theatres are always more vulnerable to physical arguments, such as fire, riots, or disease, than to charges of corrupting public morals.

The actors were clearly aware of the danger of the insidious propaganda against them and of the growing public opposition which resulted. They clung to Court protection, which proved to be fatal to their cause. In 1642 the quarrels between King and Parliament broke out into Civil War. The Parliamentary party, dominated by the Puritans, quickly captured London and the ancient hatred of the aldermen against the theatre—a hatred which had only been held in check by the patronage of the sovereign and the nobility, was at last able to wreak its revenge upon the 'rogues and vagabonds'. The religious zeal of the aldermen was strongly influenced by private interest, for the play-houses drew trade away from the merchants in the city itself, but the growing sensationalism of the plays was at least a partial excuse for the anger aroused against the players. With the Court chased out of London, the theatres were closed by Act of Parliament. The old playhouses were pulled down: the Globe in 1644, the Fortune in 1649, Blackfriars in 1655. Many of the actors were imprisoned or went into hiding. Once again the Church had struck down her irrepressible child; for eighteen years a great silence fell over the ruins of the great playhouses. Only the little carts of Thespis trudged on through the country lanes and byways, as secretly a small troupe of actors here and there performed in an old royalist's house by night, or, unnoticed by authority, amongst the busy market stalls at a country fair by day.

The French Neo-Classical Theatre

The English theatre of Shakespeare and his contemporaries reflected the aspiring mind and adventurous spirit of a heroic age—an age which had inspired the creative faculties of its playwrights and stimulated the imagination of its audience. Now it was the turn of France to experience one of those brief periods of creative genius, when suddenly the arts burst forth into a glorious summer. Athens during the latter half of the fifth century B.C. had provided the theatre with ritual and the glory of the spoken word; England, two thousand years later, had enriched it with pageantry and the character of man in action; now Italy and France were to bring about the full development of visual magic.

The new humanist learning of the Renaissance had never percolated so deeply to the people of Catholic France as it had in Protestant England. Education and the pursuit of culture had been the privilege of the court, with the result that the classical playwrights, who were widely and rudely known in Shakespeare's England, were, in France, studied and adopted with greater elegance and refinement. Whereas the English audience delighted in bloodshed and battles, the French preferred reason and psychology. But the reason and psychology, adopted by the Catholic French playwrights from the ancient pagans, had to be modified by all the advantages that the human mind had gained through Christianity and displayed with the refined taste that characterized the sermons of Bossuet and the architecture of Versailles. By psychology the French classicist meant love and gallantry; by morals he meant the behaviour of men and women in love. In France these morals were kept in reasonable bounds by the powerful influence of the Church; in England, with the example of the court to guide them, the morals of the stage were less restricted.

The French tragedies of the age of reason, though treating the classical themes, were the products of no other age or society than their own. They were written for an audience that liked to place its intellectual arguments at a safe distance from itself, thus providing them with the authority and stature which time—and particularly classical antiquity—provided. By transferring its problems to the world of antiquity, society was able to examine them with the cool detachment of reason, divorced from the vulgar intrusions of everyday life. Racine's tragedies contained many allusions to living personalities and current philosophies which were sublimated and placed in a rarefied atmosphere where they could be examined objectively. French tragedy was not popular entertainment, but an elegant, intellectual exercise which could only be appreciated by a privileged society of educated persons: the same society which glorified its king with statues dressed in classical armour and with panegyrics addressed to 'Le Roi Soleil'. The less educated English never quite appreciated this sophisticated parlour game, and most English Restoration tragedies never rose above fifth-form standards.

The first of the great classical dramatists of France, Pierre Corneille (1606–84), was the Aeschylus of French tragedy. Indeed it is strange how history appears to repeat itself, and just as Athens produced its two great tragic playwrights, Aeschylus and Sophocles, and its great comic playwright, Aristophanes, so France during its brief period of neo-classical grandeur produced Corneille, Racine, and Molière. To carry the simile still further: just as Athens produced its great debunker of the ideals of its epic age in Euripides, so France produced Voltaire who, like Euripides, was the champion of humanist thought, paving the road towards realism.

Corneille extracted French neo-classical tragedy from the confused tangles of tragi-comedy. Before his time, the French tragic stage was characterized by a form of romantic tragedy, influenced by Spanish models, especially by Cervantes and Montemayor, in which the action took place in a number of different places, and consisted of a variety of adventurous and romantic incidents imposed upon the protagonists, rather than arising naturally from their actions and character. In *Horace, Poleucte, Cinna,* and *Le Cid,* Corneille substituted progressive development, arising from a single event and leading to a logical conclusion, for the irrelevant incidents and patched-up endings which his predecessors had employed to please their public. This progressive development was called the unity of action. Like Aeschylus he chose great heroes for his characters; men and women with noble souls—who displayed no weakness or feebleness in their dealings and decisions; unlike Aeschylus, their dealings were mostly concerned with love. To match the nobility of his characters he chose larger-than-life situations and grandeur of language couched in Alexandrine verse. The conflict that Corneille developed in his tragedies was a conflict between reason and passion. Reason was usually represented by honour or duty—the son's duty to his father, the soldier's duty to the state—passion by love.

The issue of the conflict in Corneille's tragedies was never in doubt; it always ended in the victory of man over himself; it was the victory of reason. Thus Corneille embodied the ideal aim of the age of Louis XIV, in which imagination and passion were controlled and subjugated by reason. To this stern idealism Racine brought grace and sensitivity. Like Corneille he placed his action in antiquity, believing that the characters of tragedy ought to be viewed from a distance; but instead of making his characters larger than life, he made them lifelike. His characters were dominated by their passions; if they were vanquished by reason, then their defeat was the result of a bitter struggle. Racine was the champion of human reason rather than idealistic reason. He believed that tragedy should move and touch the heart of his audience, rather than impress it with elevated and rarefied idealism. Maternal sacrifice and tender sexual love in conflict with human jealousy and ambition are the themes he developed in *Andromaque, Bérénice, Phèdre, Britannicus,* and *Esther,* and his other tragedies written between 1667 and 1691. Whilst these themes might very well have produced sentimental tragedy, Racine, though sensitive, was never sentimental. His emotions were fierce and passionate; his drama was raised to the highest degree of romantic conflict from which there can be no outcome but death. But if Racine was passionate he was never melodramatic; his style was elegant, pure, simple; his management of Alexandrine verse was harmonious, and supple; like the great fugues of Bach, his plays have an almost mathematical beauty. He is the embodiment of neo-classical art, humanized by the sensitive touch of a poet.

Like Aristophanes, Molière (Jean Baptiste Poquelin, to give him his real name) approached the theatre in a very different way from the tragic playwrights of his period. He was pre-eminently a satirist, and though his comedies were written for the court, they were keenly appreciated by a popular audience; unlike Racine, Molière was essentially an actor in search of a public. The goal that he aimed at was to satirize his contemporaries: to show up their weaknesses, their absurdities, their insincerities. This he could only do by dragging them on to the stage with the costume and behaviour of their time, thus his action was placed in his own period and not in antiquity. But if Molière treated contemporary society, he was none the less classical—a product of the age of reason. He was the champion of good sense and of reason as opposed to artificiality. Those who depart from reason, like Jourdain in *Le Malade Imaginaire* or Alceste in *Le Misanthrope* end up by making themselves unhappy and ridiculous. Man must be reasonable, and above all he must seek to cultivate a balanced mind, divorced from excesses of every kind.

Whilst Molière's comedy was largely influenced by Terence who, as we have seen, was himself influenced by the Greeks, it owed even more to an indirect classical parentage—the Commedia del'Arte.

From 1570 onwards troupes of strolling players from Italy, known in France as the Comédie Italienne, had been touring the country and in due course these were invited to the court and established a permanent theatre in Paris—the Hotel de Bourgogne —which they shared with Molière's company.

The peculiarities of the Commedia were, first, that whilst the plots of the plays were written in scenario form, the dialogue was improvised; secondly, that whilst characters were stock types, like Pantelone, The Lawyer, The Spanish Captain, Arlecchino, and Pulcinella, these characters could vary to suit the peculiarities of the actor or to satirize a particular person, whose deeds or characteristics were likely to amuse the audience. Thus, the characters were constantly changing within a given framework. Some of the characters wore masks, though not all, and the staging of the plays varied from a rough booth, easily set up in the market-place or hall, to a more elaborate scenic stage on which a back-cloth was employed.

It is said that the traditions of these strolling comedians were handed down from the old Atellan mimes, but there is insufficient evidence to prove direct descent; all that can be said is that the characteristics of staging and performance were similar. To the French stage they brought a popular quality which was lacking in the classical subjects which formed the basis of the Court theatre, offering to Molière, Regnard, and Marivaux a form of satire that could be developed into literary theatre, and which, at the same time, could attract a wide audience.

Molière was himself a pupil of Scaramouche, one of the leading

Italian exponents of this popular form of theatre, and his company was trained in the traditions of the Italian comedians. From the Commedia del'Arte, Molière borrowed plots, scenes, stage-business, intrigues, and above all characters, such as Scagnarelle, modelled upon the character of the intriguing servant, Brighella. Thus, Molière's characters, for all their contemporary humanity, have about them an aura of the harlequinade; they are exaggerations of life, caricatures of the playwright's contemporaries, rather than realistic portraits. The titles of his plays—*The Miser, The Hypocrite, The Would-Be Gentleman, The Misanthropist, The Imaginary Invalid*—indicate how characters were picked out of society and exaggerated, so that they could be subjected to ridicule, which is a more entertaining and popular form of reason.

Thus, objectivity or the pursuit of reason were the guiding principles of the French stage. Imagination was kept strictly within bounds, and its limits were fixed by rules and conventions.

Racine and his contemporaries felt it necessary to tidy up the action of the play to make everything as reasonable as possible by introducing the unities of action, time, and place, which they claimed were the guiding principles of the old classical theatre. Unity of action had, in fact, been demanded by Aristotle, but the other unities were the invention of the French rationalists. Unity of place prescribed that the whole action of the play should be restricted to one locality, preferably a room, since an interior scene is easier to represent on the stage with reason than an exterior; unity of time prescribed that the events of the play should take place within twenty-four hours, though the stricter rationalists tried to make the time taken by the action coincide with the time taken by the performance.

To a great extent these unities have influenced subsequent drama; and, although the romantic theatre cast away the unities of time and place, the realistic theatre was to take them up again. Although the unity of time was more liberally interpreted and the action spread over a few days, the general tendency of the 'well-made' play was to confine the action within a limited time which did not make unreasonable demands on the imaginative flights of the audience. Gone were the specious days when the

7. 'The "mummings" of the aristocracy.'
The French Court: Ballet Joyeux de la Reine (1582).

tectum

porticus

orchestra

mimorum
ades

proscenium.

planities sive arena.

8. 'Insufficient to supply a complete answer . . .'
The Swan Theatre copied from a drawing by John de Witt (1595).

chorus of *Henry V* could call on the audience to cover vast distances and many years:

> jumping o'er times,
> Turning the accomplishment of many years
> Into an hour-glass.

The society for which Corneille, Molière, and Racine wrote demanded that the stage be as reasonable as possible if the reasonable man was to believe in, and identify himself with, the action. It did not, however, go so far as to demand that the stage should be as realistic as possible. Aristocratic society, though dominated by reason, was not lacking in imagination; it merely wished to control it. The new theatre of illusion was in fact a theatre of idealized illusion. Idealized illusion did not preclude the actors from conducting their conversation in Alexandrine couplets, from indulging in asides and expressing their thoughts in soliloquy. But it did demand that the action of the play should take place in a prescribed place, and that this place should be represented with all the visual elegance of the age.

The stage craft of the French neo-classical theatre was largely derived from Italy, where as early as the middle of the sixteenth century ballet and opera, based on classical themes, had enriched ceremonial occasions at the Italian Courts. In 1637 Sabbattini, the manager of a theatre in Pesaro, published a book on stage machinery, scenery, and lighting which revealed the remarkable inventions of the new Italian theatre of illusion. Opera and ballet had made new demands on stage-craft which the Italian masters had met with ingenuity and artistry. Scenes had to be changed rapidly: rocks had to be transformed into human beings and vice versa, ships had to be made to roll about in the sea, the heavens had to open to disgorge chariots containing gods and goddesses drawn by winged horses or dragons, thunder and lightning had to be simulated and day changed into night. In Rome, Florence, Venice, Ferrara, Naples, and Parma ballets, operas, tragedies, comedies, and pastorals were presented with increasing command of technique. French ambassadors and artists who visited the Italian courts brought back astonishing

G

descriptions of these elaborate spectacles. One of the greatest masters of the new scenic art, Giacomo Torelli, was summoned by Mazarin, chief minister to the infant Louis XIV, to display his art to the French court. Torelli was succeeded by Vigarani, father and son, and soon French authors, composers, and decorators were pressed into service and the great fêtes of Versailles became the wonder of Europe. To the rationalist mind representational scenery was necessary because it was reasonable that the play should take place somewhere, unlike the barbarous stage of the irrational Shakespeare where imagination ran wild on the stage, or the earlier French theatre where several localities were represented by a conglomeration of scenes all crowded together on the stage. Scenery had to be elegant, and it had to be idealized in order to attain classical perspective; perspective was in fact the dominant feature of scene-painting. But the idealized illusion of reality was no more realistic than the plots of the plays. The one room demanded by the unity of place, when designed by Gaspard Vigarani, the Bibiena family or Jean Bérain, was such a superb architectural concoction that it would be quite incapable of standing up had it been constructed in wood or stone, instead of being painted on a backcloth. No attempt was made to reproduce real architecture or real landscapes, nor to search into the factual details of historical costume. The palace scenes of neo-classical tragedies were represented by an all-purpose edifice —Le Palais à Volonté, as it was called, which belonged to no known period. The art of the painter, the architect, the costumier, the mechanist were brought to the service of the theatre, and never more splendidly than in the elaborate masques, fêtes, and 'divertissements' devised by the playwright, Molière, the composer, Lully, and the decorator, Jean Bérain, for the entertainment of Louis XIV.

The costumes were equally idealized; a plumed helmet and a breast-plate suggested a Roman hero, 'a forest of feathers' worn in the hat were sufficient for a tragedian, a train for a tragedienne. These stage costumes were combined with the most elegant fashions of the day. Vulgar dress was at all costs avoided; a chambermaid was dressed like a duchess, a shepherdess was adorned with ribbons and a chaplet of flowers. Thus the French theatre was, despite the introduction of visual illusion, very much or a ritual—a sophisticated ceremony to worship the Goddess of Reason, in which imagination was strictly regulated in the service of that elegant deity.

English Restoration Theatre

For eighteen years the public theatres of London remained dark. And when, in 1660, Charles II issued patents to Thomas Killigrew and Sir William Davenant to establish two playhouses in London, the popular habit of theatregoing had been broken, and the techniques and traditions, which had been consistently developed from the middle ages and which had created a unique English theatre, were largely forgotten or discarded.

Puritan propaganda had imprinted upon the public mind a deep distrust of play-acting, and this distrust was in no way mitigated by the flagrant immorality which pervaded the new playhouses and influenced the writing of the new plays. The introduction of actresses, in place of the boy-actors, and the behaviour of the Court—indeed the King himself—towards them did nothing to remove the honest citizen's distrust of the stage. The audience, which now frequented the playhouses, was a small and closed society, consisting mainly of the Court and its protégés. To this society the Elizabethan stage with its inconsistencies and inelegancies was altogether too chaotic. The old English theatre was effectively dead, and it was to France that the actors turned for their new models.

Sir William Davenant, who had been prominent amongst those who had organized the masques for the Courts of James I and his ill-fated son, was already conversant with the techniques of illusionist scenery, as well as with the machines and lighting effects which had pleased his royal masters in the past. He consequently improved upon these by adopting the other appurtenances of the new Italian and French stage-craft—the proscenium arch, orchestra pit, wings and shutters, borders and back-cloth—which had been developed to serve the gorgeous masques and fêtes of the Court of Versailles. And so the French and Italian indoor theatre of illusion with its gilded picture-frame, its front curtain, its lights, and its scenery took the place of the old English inn-yard stage.

With the new stage came, not only a new way to play old plays, but new plays of a totally different dramatic structure—plays that were modelled upon the neo-classical drama of France, even if their subject matter was drawn from the Jacobean and Cavalier theatre of England.

Thus the Restoration theatre returned from its exile like a fashionable young gentleman fresh from his travels, with his head full of the rules and disciplines that he had learnt to appreciate on the Continent. Some of these, it must be confessed, were only half understood.

In general the new English theatre was greatly inferior to its continental model. It was neither lavish enough to emulate the superb scenic effects of the new operatic tradition which Versailles had adopted from Italy and which the genius of Molière and Lully had improved; nor were the English sufficiently moved by rhymed Alexandrine verse to appreciate the classical purity of Racine's style, nor witty enough to enjoy the refinements of Molière's comedy without a liberal dose of bawdry and intrigue to add spice to the entertainment. Indeed the entertainment to be derived from a visit to a London playhouse was, as Pepys has shown, more often found in dallying with the masked courtesans in the auditorium, than by any serious involvement with the stage action. Only in one respect can the Restoration theatre claim a native individuality. This uniqueness was the stage itself, which retained something of the intimacy of the old inn-yard play-houses by projecting out beyond the picture-frame arch into the audience and thus forming an apron, flanked by doors to facilitate entrances in front of the stage proper. The Restoration theatres were provided with two doors on either side of the apron; in later Georgian theatres these were reduced to one each side. The advantage of the two doors—as Richard Southern[1] has pointed out —was that an actor could exit by one and immediately re-enter by the other. This allowed a variety of action to take place on the

[1] Changeable Scenery, Faber, 1952

apron, such as passing from one room to another, or from the outside to the inside of a building without pause. This simple convention indicates how comparatively little realism, as we know it, was employed in the early theatre of illusion. The English theatre still clung to some of the conventions of its unlocalized stage with its continuity of action. Even in the Georgian theatre the apron stage was still the main acting area and the scenery remained a background to the actors, rather than providing a confined area in which the action was expected to take place. Not until the beginning of the nineteenth century was the apron stage finally cut off and the action of the play consistently co-ordinated with the scenery. With the disappearance of the apron stage, full illusion took over from the imaginative visual participation by the audience and the revolution of stage realism became inevitable. Thus the Restoration and Georgian theatres were a half-way house between the English tradition and the continental invention.

Unlike the old inn-yard theatre, the new elegant playhouses erected in Lincoln's Inn Fields and Dorset Gardens were patronized by a small section of society. A small audience meant short runs for the plays. No play, however brilliant, could count on more than a few days' run, and a run of a week was considered a success; many plays lasted no more than one night. As in the Greek theatre, short runs resulted in productivity. A vast number of plays appeared during the period between 1660 and 1700. They were of very unequal merit.

English Restoration tragedy and tragi-comedy were evolved before Racine's influence reached our shores and were based partly on Corneille's tragedies, and partly on the heroic Jacobean drama of Middleton, Beaumont, and Fletcher, the only playwrights of the old English tradition who could be appreciated by the new taste of the Restoration public without drastic alteration. Their plots flaunted honour and an impossibly idealistic love—much the same mixture as Corneille had employed, but with the violence and bloodshed which their authors had inherited from the Jacobean playwrights. As in French tragedy, the action was removed from contemporary society, though the English tragic writers preferred more exotic locations such as Mexico, Peru, and

Morocco to the cold formalities of the Roman palaces. The principal exponents of this bombastic drama were Davenant, who mixed tragedy with music in a primitive form of opera, John Dryden, who also wrote comedies, William Boyle, Earl of Orrery, and Thomas Otway. Today the only plays that bear revival are Dryden's *All for Love* (1678) and Otway's *Venice Preserved* (1681); neither of them pure heroic tragedies, since they were not written in Alexandrine verse, which in England was never a successful medium for the stage.

The English genius did not flower at its best in following the conventions of French tragedy; it borrowed what was worse from it and ignored what was best. It used the structure and failed to appreciate the spirit of French classicism. But in comedy the English playwrights were far more successful in adapting the spirit of French comedy to a native formula. Since English taste did not appreciate the simplicity and purity of Molière, the plots that the Restoration writers borrowed from him were made more complicated; intrigue was added to intrigue. Often several of Molière's intrigues were woven together to form a network of plot, which is sometimes difficult to follow. Restoration comedy, too, borrowed freely from Ben Jonson and other playwrights of the Jacobean school, pressing their diffuse action into a unity of action with far greater success than was achieved in the adaptations of tragedy. Restoration society provided the comic playwrights with ample material to satirize; for, whilst heroic tragedy was almost devoid of inspiration, since heroism was dead and virtue non-existent, the English comedy of manners, which now came to its full growth, had plenty of manners to inspire it—albeit not very savoury ones.

The comedies of William Congreve, John Dryden, William Wycherley, Sir George Etherege, Sir John Vanbrugh, and George Farquhar are among the most brilliant in the literature of the English stage, though it must be added that they are totally lacking in morality and no less lacking in warm humanity. Congreve in *Love for Love* (1695) and *The Way of the World* (1700) attained a literary brilliance with a cold, hard view of humanity which epitomized the courtly society of his age, with its insincerities and heartless amours, its intrigues and scandals. Wycherley in *The Country Wife* (1674–5) shows the inherited coarseness which he derived from Jonson and other Jacobean writers, mixed with a highly sophisticated and entertaining humour. In *The Man of Mode or Sir Fopling Flutter* (1676), Etherege caricatured the fop of the age with his exaggerations of dress, behaviour, and language. The popularity of this stage character caused a repetition of fops to appear throughout the comedies of the late seventeenth and eighteenth centuries. Vanbrugh in *The Provoked Wife* (1697) and Farquhar in *The Recruiting Officer* and *The Beaux Stratagem* (1707) carry their intrigues into the country, where a slight breath of humanity softens the hard, brittle chatter of St. James's Park and the Mall.

Shakespeare was still played in the Restoration theatres, but to the mind of the reasonable man his wild notes needed taming, and his profusion of scenes and characters was accordingly pruned and trimmed by the dramatists and actors of the late seventeenth century to fit the convention of the theatre of idealized illusion. Nicholas Rowe added suitable stage directions and patched up the unspecified scene-titles with scenic locations, such as 'Another part of the wood'. Sir William Davenant, Edward Howard, and Nahum Tate in an excess of reasonable tidiness obliged with new endings to Shakespeare's plays. In *King Lear*, for instance, Cordelia was happily married off to Edgar. *Macbeth* was 'classicized' by Otway, *Antony and Cleopatra* and *The Tempest* by Dryden, *Timon of Athens* by Shadwell. The language was made simpler; imagery was discarded; scenes were unified; comic scenes were edited and contemporary, and often indecent, language was introduced; heroes were made more heroic; tragedies and comedies given a political—which meant a strongly royalist—slant. Such lack of appreciation of the outlook and aesthetics of a society which differed from their own is to be found in later ages, and it would be wrong to judge the age of Congreve and Dryden because it failed to understand an age when verbal imagery took the place of visual illusion and when imagination was more important than logic.

CHAPTER TEN

ARTIFICIAL ACTING

THE PERFORMANCE OF RESTORATION COMEDY

THEATRE is the reflection of contemporary society. To perform a Restoration comedy in our contemporary theatre we must seek to capture the style of the society that it reflects.

The society which patronized the Theatre Royal (Drury Lane) and the theatres of Lincoln's Inn Fields or Dorset Gardens was no longer inspired by the discoveries, adventures, and ideals of Elizabethan England. Unlike the supremely self-confident society inspired by the golden sun that reigned over France, Charles II's England was conscious of its decadence. Thus Restoration tragedy is an artificial creation; its style is hollow and bombastic compared with the exaltation of French tragedy. Restoration tragedy sought after exoticism, rather than purity; the titles of the tragedies indicate a taste for the bizarre: *The Cruelty of the Spaniards in Peru, The Indian Emperor or the Conquest of Mexico, Aureng-Zebe, Constantine the Great, The Conquest of Granada by the Spaniards*. Although Restoration comedy reflects the attitude of a tiny society isolated from the great mass of the people, aware of the shock it caused to their puritanical outlook and contemptuous of the criticism it aroused, it has the merit of being a genuine reflection of that society. This minority society, for all its hollowness and lack of morals, cultivated wit and elegance which, as reflected in the major comedies of the period, should overcome our moral scruples—if we have them—and provide us today with comedies that enrich an adult theatre.

In no other form of theatre is the cult of naturalism so out of place as in the performance of the sophisticated comedies of Congreve and his contemporaries. To attempt to impose naturalistic acting or décor upon them is to destroy totally the effect of their style. To produce these plays today we must start with the stage itself. A fore-stage with doors in front of the proscenium arch would seem to be desirable, since the actors should act in front of the scenery rather than inside it if the artificial style of Restoration acting is to be discovered. Those characteristics of naturalism, such as realistic noises off, pauses, and pregnant silences, have no place in the artificialities of the period. The effect must be of performance *in front* of a picture or a formal architectural arrangement, and not *within* a picture-frame; of lightness of choreography, of quickness of eye and of ear. Furniture and properties should be confined to the essential requirements of the action and the placing of these upon the stage must be formal in design. In a naturalistic interior we place our sofas and tables where they are best suited to the action of the play and most easily accessible to the actors. In a Restoration interior the furniture should be placed from the point of view of its effect to emphasise the formality of the scene.

The acting of this artificial comedy requires a particular approach which differs from the approach we make to tragedy or drama or, indeed, to the human comedies of Tchekhov. It demands, too, accurate technique and timing.

In Restoration comedy we are not dealing with highly complex human beings; we are not asked to make a deep analysis of motivation nor to discover hidden emotions and feelings. The characters of artificial comedy are generalizations of humanity; they are surface types of the human species whose characteristics are displayed by the actor by surface means much as he would imitate the characteristics and behaviour of a bird or a butterfly.

The actor and actress playing Sir John and Lady Brute in *The Provoked Wife* would not approach these characters with the same degree of involvement as they would the characters of Torvald and Nora in *The Doll's House*. They would stand a little aside from the characters and study their antics. It is the surface behaviour of the characters that has to be studied and displayed with all the interpretive invention that comes from an exact study of the manners and outlook of the period. So, a study and feeling for period is more essential and requires a greater degree of accuracy in artificial comedy than in any other form of comedy or drama because these generalizations are not just generalizations of human beings in all ages, but of human beings of one particular age and of one particular section of society. They cannot successfully be transferred to another period and acted in terms of another type of society. Thus whilst the characters are generalizations of humanity, the particular form of humanity was one that behaved in a very specialized way and according to a very precise code of etiquette. The actor must first absorb the outlook of the particular society which constitutes the basis of the Restoration high-society comedy. This is an artificial code of behaviour created to cloak inner feelings, designed to serve the selfish interests and particular outlook of a small section of the community. Anything which lies outside this section is made to appear unbalanced, bizarre, and foolish. Thus, the merchant, the country-squire, the parson, the old coquette, the elderly husband, the miser, the misanthropist, the prude, and so on, are figures of fun; whereas the man of the world who succeeds in concealing his emotions and his amours, who indulges in no excess of virtue or of vice, whose head rules his heart and who is always perfectly poised and controlled, is regarded as the model of good breeding.

Etiquette, rather than virtue or vice, is the yardstick by which the code of behaviour is measured and comedy arises when the characters exceed or fall short of this yardstick. The actor, then, must first understand and absorb what is meant by etiquette in Restoration society—and this concerns not only the sort of outlook mentioned above, but, no less, the manners, behaviour, speech, movement, dress, habits, and all the external characteristics of the age. The technique required of the actor to master these external characteristics is of paramount importance. The main emphasis of acting must be placed on rhythm and timing, precision of movement, stance, and gesture. The choreography of movement must be carefully studied so that a living pattern is created by the actors emphasizing the rhythm of the text and pointing the lines, rather than arising from any naturalistic impulse. Stance is important, since the actors will spend most of their time on their feet, not lounging in armchairs or lying on their faces on a sofa. The management of properties, such as swords, sticks, and hats, must be elegant and accomplished; we must never feel that these are strange and awkward encumbrances thrust upon the actor by the designer. The speaking of the lines is all important, and here the actor must know how to sense their values—the rhythm of their cadences, their tempo, and their climaxes; their shades of meaning must be studied as if they were part of a musical score. In the Restoration theatre, music played a vital role. Many of the tragedies were set to music, such as *Macbeth* and *The Tempest*; Davenant and Dryden wrote dramatic operas, and songs were liberally interspersed in the comedies. The music of Purcell, Lully, Monteverdi, Alessandro Scarlatti, and even later composers such as Bach, Handel, and Arne can lead us towards the feeling for the rhythm and tempos required by the highly rhythmic prose. To hear Molière spoken by the company of the Comédie française is to hear verbal music, and this musical speech is the result of long and meticulous training.

One of the worst mistakes in attempting to reproduce the style of the Restoration theatre is to confuse elegance with archness. There is nothing coy or arch about the ladies of Wycherley or Congreve. Restoration ladies of fashion as well as the gallants were flagrantly immodest and boldly provocative; there was no such thing as a man of virtue, nor an innocent woman either. So the study of character is mainly concerned with the study of the outlook and characteristics of the period. In performing such types as Sir Novelty Fashion or Sir Tunbelly Clumsy the actor must be able to assume a double role. He must both enter into the character and stand outside it, to share the joke, as it were, with his audience. This dual action is much the same as that of a raconteur who tells a funny story to his friends which requires both involvement and detachment; it is not the same as the action of the actor of a dramatic character in a play by Ibsen who is largely unconscious of his audience and is exclusively concerned with living his part. Success in the acting of a type will depend not only on our ability to see and create the eccentricity or off-balance behaviour of the type, but on our ability to convey our enjoyment of this eccentricity to the audience. For truth in artificial comedy is not truth but a caricature of it. The audience does not require to believe in Lady Wishfort or Lord Foppington as real human beings, but it does require to believe in the truthfulness of our caricature of an old coquette and an old fop, and not merely of any old coquette and fop, but of a particular type of these eccentrics in a particular epoch of history.

Thus the actor of Restoration comedy must acquire great accuracy in his delineation of manners, speech, behaviour, and movement if the caricature is to be immediately recognized and accepted.

If acting a Restoration comedy is largely a matter of technique, rather like a game of tennis, in which footwork, rhythm, quick brain, and good co-ordination are essential, it is also a matter of feeling. We must savour the situations, the affectations, the atmosphere of intrigue, even the bawdiness, and not least, we must understand and demonstrate the aristocracy of the play's conception and the contemptuous effrontery of the age. An age in which the common man, be he citizen or country-squire, was despised; in which anyone who was anyone knew each other, so that no secrets were hid and no vices unknown. An age which, for all its affectation, was essentially frank about itself.

CHAPTER ELEVEN

THE GROWTH OF ILLUSION

THEATRE DURING THE EIGHTEENTH CENTURY

THE theatre of the age of reason was largely the pursuit of a leisured class. Its hey-day coincided with an age when the Court was almost the only wealthy and cultural force in society. It was in fact a Court theatre, exclusively confined to the society of the capital cities. But this leisured class which considered work the function of lesser beings soon lost its wealth in the extravagances of Court life and the gambling table. Wealth spread to the merchants, both in the capital and in the great English provincial cities, where theatres under Royal patents began to appear. With wealth came the urge to imitate the aristocratic way of life, but with this difference, that the bourgeois audience wanted sentimental not salacious plays and domestic not classical situations. The imagination of the corn merchant could not be stirred by the heroics of Alexandrine verse; and his good wife was profoundly shocked by the spicy epigrams of the Restoration wits.

In 1697 Jeremy Collier, filled with Puritan zeal, issued an attack on the dramatists in his *A Short View of the Immorality and Profaneness of the English Stage*. In his attack, which was courageous and in many ways justified, he made the mistake of accusing the stage of corrupting the morals of society, instead of realizing that the stage was—as it always is—not a teacher, but a reflection of society itself. The attack found its mark and did much to bring about the reforms which encouraged a larger bourgeois audience to visit the theatre.

But, if immorality on the stage was distasteful to the bourgeoisie, the achievement of a place in high society was still their dream-wish; and, whilst the good merchants were anxious to cleanse the stage of vice and show virtue triumphant, they were also anxious to preserve the fashionable tone of the plays and the elegant externals of deportment. Comedy was sentimentalized and purified, tragedy turned into domestic melodrama.

This change in the nature of the plays discouraged the Court wits and their protégés from writing for the theatre. With few exceptions they withdrew and their place was taken by hack writers who knew more precisely what the new audience wanted. There were, however, exceptions to this reign of nonentities. In France Marivaux and Beaumarchais managed to meet the require-ments of the larger and more squeamish public, whilst still retaining wit. In England John Gay, Oliver Goldsmith, and Richard Brinsley Sheridan let off some joyous fireworks to illuminate the rather dismal squibs of sentimental domestic comedy. Goldsmith's *She Stoops to Conquer* (1773) skilfully combines the homely manners of country life with the fashionable behaviour of the city gentleman, including only a hint at those loose Court morals which shocked the middle-class public. Even in Sheridan's *The School for Scandal* (1777) the worst that happens is the discovery of Lady Teazle hiding behind a screen. *The Rivals* (1775) is a purely sentimental plot strengthened by some glorious characterization. In it Sheridan clearly shows his intention—and a sound business-like intention it seemed—to use the material of the notorious Restoration plays, but to clean them up so as to give no possible offence to his bourgeois public. This principle he pursued in *The Critic,* an adaptation of Buckingham's *Rehearsal,* and in *A Trip to Scarborough,* a genteel version of Vanbrugh's *Relapse.* The plots of these plays are easy to follow by the simplest intellect, which is more than can be said for the complicated intrigues of Congreve's *The Way of the World,* and *Love for Love,* where it is difficult to know what is happening. Unfortunately his success as a playwright was not matched by his success as a theatre manager. After an unsuccessful career as manager and shareholder of Drury Lane he deserted the theatre for the lesser responsibilities of the House of Commons.

Whilst Restoration theatre was characterized by its exclusive aristocratic audience—an audience that was entirely confined to London—the citizens' theatre of the eighteenth century broadened the basis of the metropolitan audiences and reached out to the provincial cities, as well as to Dublin and Edinburgh.

Illusion was increased to compensate for the poor quality of the plays as well as to cater for the lower imaginative level of the business-man and his spouse, and to this end the stages were enlarged and their equipment improved. A new system of lighting the stage from the sides took the place of the chandeliers which were suspended above it—irrespective of whether the scene was laid in a palace, a tomb, or in the countryside. Privileged playgoers, who had been accustomed to sit at the sides of the stage were banished in France by Voltaire and in England by Garrick. Scenery became more real, stage costume became more diverse, although it was some time before the actors—and more especially the actresses—showed any real inclination to abandon their finery and adopt a dress suitable to their characters. The citizen's spouse came to the theatre to see high life and good manners, and when Garrick played Macbeth he mightily displeased his public by appearing 'in one of his scenes of greatest confusion . . . with his coat and waistcoat unbuttoned and with some other discomposures in his dress'. A fault that he later rectified to please his public.

> The Drama's laws, the Drama's patrons give,
> For we that live to please, must please to live,

wrote Dr. Johnson in a prologue to one of Garrick's plays.

But gradually, as travel and knowledge spread, greater attention was paid to antique costume and the dress of foreign lands. In 1773 Macklin even went so far as to abandon the gold-braided scarlet suit, in which Macbeth always appeared, and dressed himself from head to foot in a tartan attire. His entrance was appropriately heralded by the playing of the Coldstream March.

Acting remained strictly formal. Manner was more cultivated than passion, for the vulgar gestures and habits of everyday life were completely foreign to the ritual of the eighteenth-century stage. Goethe, who after a wild excursion into romanticism returned to direct the neo-classical theatre of the Weimar Court, summarized the principles of acting thus:

First of all, the player must consider that he should not only imitate nature but also portray it ideally, thereby, in his presentation, uniting the true and the beautiful.

He also provided some useful hints on the niceties of stage deportment:

The actor should not produce a handkerchief on the stage, nor blow his nose or spit. It is terrible, within the sphere of a work of art, to be reminded of such physical necessities.

Into this schoolroom of decorum little David Garrick (1717–97) came bounding like a coloured ball thrown through the window by the vulgar children in the street outside. Thus Richard Cumberland describes how he first saw Garrick in Nicholas Rowe's *The Fair Penitent*:

. . . but when after long and eager expectation I first beheld little Garrick, then young and light and alive in every muscle and in every feature, come bounding on the stage . . . heavens, what a transition! it seemed as if a whole century had been swept over in the transition of a single scene; old things were done away, and a new order at once brought forward, bright and luminous, and clearly destined to dispel the barbarisms and bigotry of a tasteless age, too long attached to the prejudices of custom, and superstitiously devoted to the illusions of imposing declamation.

But, whilst a greater degree of illusion was introduced to cater for the imaginative level of the bourgeois audience, this illusion was still far from being realistic. Good manners and the niceties of behaviour were the ideals of bourgeois society—ideals that soon degenerated into artificialities. The titles of the plays give an indication of the pervading taste: *The London Merchant, The Citizens' Wives in the Fashion, The Citizens of Quality, The Clandestine Marriage*. The good citizen and his wife, dreaming of the day when their daughter—endowed with a fat dowry—would be married off to an impoverished peer, were able to identify themselves with this sentimental and artificial vision of aristocratic life.

Yet sinister forces were at work to undermine the complacent life of the community and its ideals of order and establishments. Doubts began to be expressed about the unities of time and place. Dr. Johnson very aptly pointed out that in the theatre we do not believe ourselves to be in a room anyway; and, if we can imagine ourselves to be in a room at one moment, we can imagine ourselves to be somewhere else at the next. The whole social structure of aristocratic drama with its heroes drawn from the royal houses of ancient literature, from exotic eastern courts or from the fashionable society of London, was lampooned by John Gay in *The Beggar's Opera* and by Beaumarchais in *Le Barbier de Seville*, whose barber hero was looked upon as a dangerous symbol of political chaos. During the arguments which surrounded the refusal of the authorities to permit the production of his play Beaumarchais is said to have declared to Louis XVI that he would bring down the Bastille, rather than see his play kept off the stage. The play did not bring down the Bastille, but the society that applauded it did.

When the Bastille fell and the whole façade of establishments and estates of the age of reason crashed to the ground, imagination came bursting out from its confines. As we look back at the development of the architecture of the eighteenth century, we can suppose the imprisoned imagination crawling up the Corinthian pillars and burgeoning from the cornices of the symmetrical palaces and churches, as the romantic elaborations grew over the classical buildings. Their weight brought the façades tumbling down in the ruins of revolution.

The Romantic Theatre

The scene now shifts to Germany, where during the last decades of the eighteenth century the *Sturm und Drang* movement led the theatre's revolt against the *ancien régime*. Inspired by Johann Wolfang von Goethe and Friedrich Schiller, the romantics upheld the divine right of the individual against the conventions of society, espoused Rousseau's doctrine of nature, and violently

H

assaulted Racine's fortress of reason and the bourgeois sentimentalism that had grown like ivy around it. The unities of time and place were cast to the wind. Scene followed scene—the wilder and more exotic the better. Years rolled by in the course of a few hours, and down went the improbable edifice of the *palais à volonté*. Rebellion, rape, and murder, as well as the mysteries of the supernatural, rampaged through plays like Goethe's *Faust Part One*, Schiller's *Die Räuber*, H. L. Wagner's *Die Kindesmörderin*, and the intolerable melodramas of Kotzebue, who wrote no less than two hundred plays, many of which won enormous popularity in London.

The movement spread throughout Europe. It was less successfully reflected in the literary drama of England by Byron's *Manfred* and Shelley's *The Cenci*, but it found liberal exercise in the popular melodramas which left the spectators gaping with amazement as Vesuvius erupted or the heroine was hurled headlong into the boiling cauldron of the mill-race.

Even in France, the home of sweet reason, Victor Hugo and Alexandre Dumas shook the confident traditions of the Comédie française with *Hernani* (1830), *Ruy Blas* and *Henri III et sa Cour*, and Dumas's *La Tour de Nesle* (1832) surpassed any play so far seen in the French theatre in its sustained terror and the mounting pile of its corpses.

Shakespeare was the hero of the day; and, for the first time, he became an international dramatist. His plays were translated into German by August Wilhelm Schlegel. They were praised and imitated by the French.

The romantic actors abandoned formal declamation, the niceties of deportment, the buskin and the feathers and the *grande toilette*. They performed with passion and terror in the barbaric costumes of the past. 'To see Kean act,' said Coleridge, 'was to read Shakespeare by flashes of lightning'.

The difference between the classical manner and the romantic was summarized by Leigh Hunt in a comparison between Kemble, the exponent of classical acting, and Kean, the great romantic.

The distinction between Kean and Kemble may be briefly stated to be this: that Kemble knew there was a difference between tragedy and common life, but did not know in what it consisted, except in *manner*, which he consequently carried to excess, losing sight of the passion. Kean knows the real thing, which is the height of the *passion*. . . . Kemble began with the flower, and he made it accordingly. He had no notion of so inelegant a thing as a root, or as the common earth, or of all the precious elements that make a heart and a life in the plant, and crown their success with beauty . . . Kean's face is full of light and shade, his tones vary, his voice trembles, his eye glistens, sometimes with withering scorn, sometimes with a tear: at least he can speak as if there were tears in his eyes, and he brings tears into those of other people.

Kean brought more than tears to the eyes of Byron, who fainted at his distorted face and distracted aspect in *A New Way to Pay Old Debts*.

The scene-painters, the stage mechanics, and the lighting experts struggled valiantly to keep up with the public demand for spectacular illusion. Romantic castles, ruins, ravines, gloomy dungeons, tempestuous seas, trap doors, gauzes, moving dioramas lit by flickering gaslight were brought into service. Flames and smoke, thunder and lightning, horses and deer, and even elephants, attempted to satisfy the greedy appetite of a public accustomed to a diet of the severed heads of its rulers and the carnage of Waterloo.

The excessive demand for illusion and spectacle resulted in the ascendancy of the scenic technician, and once again the artist-playwright retired from the theatre. Goldsmith turned to novel-writing, Sheridan to politics, Goethe, after a cooling-off visit to Italy, turned back to the classicism of *Iphigenia in Aulis*, horrified by the excesses of the creature he had unleashed. Frankenstein's monster became the master, instead of the servant, of its creator.

CHAPTER TWELVE

THE MATERIALIST THEATRE

MELODRAMA AND SPECTACLE

THE French Revolution did more than release the imagination which had for so long been guided and shaped by the taste of an aristocratic society; it broke the strings that held society together by taking away the kingpins around which it revolved. The spread of democracy split society into a number of units, and from now on we can no longer talk of a single cultural force which controlled the outlook of the audience and dictated the style of the stage. Moreover, a more powerful and far-reaching revolution than that which brought down the Bastille was taking place; especially in England—the Industrial Revolution.

During the first seventy-five years of the nineteenth century the British theatre underwent a profound change, and in the process it sank to an undistinguished level unequalled in its history. There were many causes for this, but chief among them were the new opportunities of making money. The Industrial Revolution offered opportunities of wealth to new sections of the community; it brought into the cities—and especially into London —a vast working-class population, which was a ready prey to the purveyors of cheap drink and cheap entertainment. It nurtured a new industrial wealthy class which, lacking the traditions and taste of the older leaders of public opinion, wanted easy entertainment at a low intellectual level.

In all ages the theatre has embraced showmanship, but in no age was its manifestation so given over to the almost exclusive cult of vulgarity as during the early and mid-Victorian period. Heavy melodrama liberally spiced with sensational spectacle, beery burlesque, and low music-hall, catered for the taste of the illiterate working class; whilst farce, lacking in both wit and humour, and sentimental and banal drama, hypocritically praising the virtues of poverty and righteous living, offered a comforting post-prandial cordial to the new rich.

The enormous increase in the population of London was reinforced by the development of the railways which made it possible for provincial people to visit the London theatres more easily and frequently. These two factors had important consequences: the theatres were increased in size and the type of play produced was on the whole chosen to suit the taste of the lowest common denominator in the large and often illiterate audiences. Spectacle was almost essential in the large theatres owing to their size, and every imaginable stage decoration and device was brought into service, often irrespective of any relevance to the style or subject-matter of the plays. The tendency to elaborate plays with music and spectacle, and to alter their texts to accommodate these introductions, was further encouraged by the legal regulations that restricted the playing of straight plays to the two licensed playhouses—Drury Lane and Covent Garden. These Patent theatres, which bore the prefix 'Theatre Royal', were the only theatres entitled to sell tickets for plays, though the Haymarket was also permitted to do so during the summer months. The enormously increased demand for entertainment encouraged the managements of the unlicensed theatres to adopt every ruse to get round the legal restrictions. A favourite method was to disguise plays as burlettas, operettas, varieties, and extravaganzas by introducing incidental music and not less than six songs into the action. Thus the Surrey Theatre managed to produce in one year *Antony and Cleopatra, The Beaux Stratagem, The Merry Wives of Windsor, King Lear,* and *Richard III* with hotchpotch musical accompaniments and a selection of unsuitable songs. The development of musical plays and extravaganzas had, however, one happy result, as it produced the cult of the pantomime—an exclusively English form of theatrical entertainment.

The monopoly of the Patent Theatres was not broken until 1843, when the Act for Regulating the Theatres was passed.

This long overdue measure was, however, introduced too late to have any immediate effect, for by this time public taste had degenerated. The theatre was no longer judged as an art, merely as a 'show' in which spectacle, frivolity, and a minimum of mental effort were demanded of the audience. In their eagerness to make money, and spurred on by the pressure of competition for the public's favour, the managements and actors found no use for good authorship. Playwriting became a formula in which the same ingredients were repeated again and again, so long as they still drew a public. Thus the best writers of the day found no place in the theatre. Wordsworth, Coleridge, Shelley, Keats, Byron and later Browning, Tennyson, and Swinburne wrote poetic plays for the study, and the British theatre lost playwrights who, had they worked for the theatre, might have provided a new golden age.

The major influence on drama, apart from spectacle, came from France where Victorien Sardou, Eugène Scribe, Casimir Bonjour, Emile Augier, and the younger Dumas were providing a society, weary of the excesses of the revolutionary romantics, with 'well-made' bourgeois plays which reflected the money-conscious and highly conventional outlook of Paris during the reign of Louis-Philippe and Napoleon III. Casimir Bonjour's *Money: or the Manners of the Age* (1826), Sardou's *Scrap of Paper* (1860) and *Diplomacy* (1877), Dumas' *Lady of the Camellias* (1852), were successfully presented in London and provided models for the plays of Bulwer Lytton, Sir Henry Taylor, and Dion Boucicault. The plays of Victorien Sardou (1831–1908) are perhaps the most blatant examples of commercialism that the age produced. The playwright regarded his plays purely as vehicles for making money. It cannot be denied that he was a cunning maker of plays, fitting his pieces together into a pattern calculated to hold a well-dined audience's attention without undue effort, but his characters were totally lacking in life and his situations bore no relation to truth. In Paris, his plays were usually performed by the great French actress, Sarah Bernhardt, and no doubt appeared to be better than they were, but the fact that these plays were highly regarded in literate circles in London is proof of the general decadence of taste amongst the self-styled leaders of public opinion. This new type of 'well-made' sentimental play, which mixed melodrama with a highly materialistic plot, was labelled by Shaw 'Sardoodledum'. Despite its poverty of ideas and lack of artistic integrity, the 'well-made' play was nevertheless to become the beginning of the realistic theatre; and despite the scorn with which Shaw and the later nineteenth-century playwrights regarded the sentimentality of the early materialist school, there is a direct line of descent from the 'well-made' play of Sardou to the early Shavian comedies—what was lacking was good playwrights, and above all playwrights with integrity.

Side by side with the 'well-made' melodrama of the materialist playwrights, romantic melodrama flourished throughout the century. Such pieces as Boucicault's *Colleen Bawn* (1860), *The Streets of London*, and *Maria Marten or Murder in the Red Barn*, have no merit today other than to provoke our laughter at their ludicrous sentiments and naïve plots, but the burlesques and fairy plays of J. R. Planché, which were so popular in the theatres between 1818 and 1872, were to provide the basis upon which Gilbert and Sullivan constructed their operettas, and musical-comedy owes its origins to these mixtures of dance, song, scenery, and sentimental story.

The Actor-Manager's Theatre

Romanticism, historical-realism, and melodrama were all mixed together in the spectacular productions of the actor-managers. The highly coloured performances of Shakespeare which Charles Kean, son of the great romantic actor, Edmund Kean, presented at the Princess Theatre between 1851 and 1859 started a new phase of theatre management, in which the leading actor assumed dictatorial control. This phase—the actor-manager's theatre—was to dominate the English theatre for good and ill during the second half of the century. For good, in that the actor-managers raised the level of the acting profession and improved the techniques of the stage; for ill, in that they tended to exclude contemporary writers of merit, relying too heavily on spectacle and on plays containing parts which emphasized their own powers of virtuoso performance. To this end they ruthlessly cut and altered Shakespeare's texts to place the maximum emphasis on their own roles and to decorate their stage with as much spectacle as possible.

The habit of tailoring Shakespeare's plays was not new— it had been practised since the Restoration—but the new stage improvements introduced in a scientific and machine age allowed displays of extraneous spectacle to turn them into romantic melodrama. Charles Kean and his successors placed great store on historical accuracy. Books of heraldry and archaeology were searched for details of historical costumes, armour, coats of arms, and properties. Scene painters were despatched to Rome and Athens to sketch the landscape and reconstruct on the stage the buildings of ancient times. Horses and chariots, crowd scenes and embattled armies were introduced to provide a lively picture and to create an illusion of reality in place of Shakespeare's call upon the imagination.

'Think when we talk of horses, that you see them . . .' was not at all to the taste of the mid-Victorian playgoer. Materialism had destroyed the imaginative receptiveness of London society as it had done in the days of the Roman Empire.

In the hands of the actor-manager, this mixture of romance, melodrama, and realism in the form of historical accuracy was the highest form of theatrical art that the British stage produced during the greater part of the century. Its weakness was that it was too often dependent on one, or at most two, isolated performances to transcend acting material which was often second-rate. The actor-managers tended to over-emphasize the major roles to the detriment of the plays as a whole, and to dissipate their energies and fortunes on spectacular scenic illusion. This tendency to overreach themselves, and their lack of restraint both in their personal performance and in their staging, usually resulted in a brief moment of glory followed by a tragic end in penury.

The greatest of the actor-managers was Henry Irving who managea the Lyceum Theatre in London from 1878 to 1901. His first great success was achieved in *The Bells*, an adaptation of a French melodrama by Erckmann-Chatrian, which today seems to be slightly ludicrous in its highly coloured theatricality. At the Lyceum he was partnered by one of the best actresses of the British theatre, Ellen Terry, and around his magnetic personality there gathered a team of talented actors, painters, and archaeologists. His productions were always presented with considerable lavishness, which disguised the poverty of many of the dramatic scripts he used. For although Irving presented many of Shakespeare's plays, the rest of his repertoire consisted of plays more remarkable for the extravagant opportunities they offered to the leading actor than for their artistic and dramatic merits. *The Corsican Brothers, Richlieu, Louis XI, A Story of Waterloo,* and *Madame Sans Gêne* are typical of the romantic, historical melodrama favoured by the actor-managers. Irving's own acting style was intense and hypnotic, and for this reason he tended to choose parts that displayed a larger than life dimension. Often the characters he drew were slightly mad or psychological curiosities. Such outsize parts suited his long, pale face, burning eyes, halting gait, and peculiar pronunciation. Yet, despite his much criticized mannerisms, Irving gave back to the London theatre its lost magnificence; he did much to re-establish the dignity of his profession and to overcome the Puritan prejudice against it.

The Long-run Theatre

Before we consider the revolt against Romanticism which began whilst Irving was still perpetuating the Romantic style, we must turn back to earlier events in the century which were to influence this movement. We have seen how economic factors and the development of travel facilities had brought larger and less discriminating audiences to the theatre; and how this, in turn, produced a degeneration in the quality of the plays, and an increase in spectacle and 'show business'. There were to be further consequences. Larger audiences meant the possibility of longer runs for the plays, and in time this was to bring about the dissolution of the old repertory system and the disbanding of the stock companies. From the days of Shakespeare onwards, British actors had performed their plays in what is today called the 'continental' repertory system. By this system each theatre had a stock of plays and these were changed nightly in the same way as the operatic repertoire. This system operated both in London and in many patent theatres in the provinces. The stock companies which performed these plays were engaged for the season and often for longer, and consequently the system ensured a reasonably permanent livelihood to the actors. Although the productions were lacking in perfection, and although scenery and costumes had to be reduced to the simplest, the performance of a variety of plays by actors constantly playing together developed versatility and a form of ensemble-playing among the actors which could only be achieved by many weeks of rehearsal and performance in the long-run theatre which followed it. But perhaps the most important advantage of this system was that, since it did not necessitate that every play in the repertoire should be a box-office success, it allowed plays to be performed that would otherwise not have been seen. To some extent the stronger plays could support the weaker ones, and, whilst a weak play might have to be withdrawn from performance or performed only seldom, the same disastrous consequences did not result from the failure of a play in the stock system as resulted from the failure of a play which was put on for a long run. A healthy theatre is largely dependent upon its flow of new plays. A theatre which is too dependent upon success becomes too fearful of new work. George Devine, in championing the cause of experiment today, has referred to this as 'the right to fail'. A theatre which cannot afford this right eventually loses its vitality.

The temptation of high profits resulting from the larger audiences produced the long-run system. It is to be remembered to the credit of the actor-managers that, despite their personal popularity which might have allowed them to perform their plays for long runs, they frequently maintained the stock system, often to their financial detriment.

With the decay of the stock system, the acting profession was reduced to casual labour and greater power was concentrated in the hands of the manager. High profits, too, encouraged the theatrical speculator who had little interest in anything outside the money-making potentialities of show business. The attitude of the theatre towards the playwright—and more particularly towards the true artist—became increasingly cautious, if not hostile; when eventually writers like Shaw, Ibsen, and Tchekhov arose they could find no commercial management in London to present their work.

With wider and more powerful means of mass communication came an increase in the reputation and value of the 'star' actors, and a fortune could be won by the impresarios or speculators who could secure their services. The tendency to place the value of the actor above the value of the play is inherent in Romanticism and was exaggerated by materialism. The 'star system' operated to the detriment of the performance as a whole no less than to the detriment of the playwright, for theatre came largely to be valued by the reputations of its 'star' actors rather than by the conception of it as a total art.

This led to abuses which have never been totally eradicated. The cult of the leading actor is inherent in the nature of theatre and it would clearly be against nature to deny the right of the public to value the merits of a great actor and to see him perform in plays which offered scope for his talents. It is the exploitation of this natural aspect of theatre that produces abuses of theatrical art, and, where the profit motive is uppermost, the temptations are greatest.

Thus the advent of a materialist theatre which offered high profits to the successful and unscrupulous brought about a general degeneration of theatre itself and in the public's attitude towards it. Vulgar showmanship, unbalanced performance, and a decline in the critical faculties of the audience were the results.

CHAPTER THIRTEEN

THE THEATRE OF ACTUALITY

THE BIRTH OF REALISM

Realistic Techniques

UNDER the surface of the materialist degeneration were the seeds of important changes: the realistic theatre as we know it today was gradually being conceived. Slowly but surely the improvement in the techniques of production, scenery, and lighting were to bring about a more lifelike performance. To this end the introduction of gaslight in the London theatres in 1817 had far-reaching consequences; for not only could the auditorium lights be extinguished, but the stage lights could be regulated in intensity. At first the effects of this new lighting appeared to be too bright in comparison with the gentler glow of candles and oil lamps, but gradually with the invention of 'blinds of coloured cloth' to alter the colour of the light and the independent control of each lamp by means of 'the gas table' (an early form of central lighting control), this new system offered increasing possibilities of suggesting a greater illusion of reality.

But, perhaps, the most important effect of gaslighting was that, by reason of its greater brightness and because it could be adjusted to cover any given area of the stage, the movement of the actors became more flexible. The ability of the actor to move freely about the stage in depth as well as in width was increased by the invention of the incandescent limelight which could follow him wherever he went. Previously the row of oil footlights or candles in the front of the stage and the chandeliers hanging above it had made the 'down-stage', or front of the stage, the only part which could be effectively lit. Consequently movement had been largely restricted to a straight line across the front of the apron-stage. Now, for the first time, it was possible to move in depth and still permit the actor's face to be seen by the audience. This encouraged far more movement to take place, and the positioning and moves of the actors became more close to real life and required greater attention at rehearsal. Increased reality in movement and lighting necessitated the services of someone to work out the details of the performance and to observe their effect from the front of the house. The old habit of keeping six feet away from the leading actor who stood manfully in the centre of the stage was dying out. Acting became more complicated and closer to life.

At the same time as these lighting improvements were increasing the realism of movement, the shape of the stage itself was being altered. The apron stage with its side-doors, which had been the main acting area, was no longer required once the actors were free to manœuvre in depth. The stage could now become a box framed by the proscenium arch and the actors could act in the scenery and not in front of it. Thus the scenery now became an integral part of the action instead of a background to it, with the result that it, too, became more real in structure. It also became more elaborate; for, with the long-run plays, it was possible to stage the scenes with much greater elaboration than in the stock theatres with their nightly change of bill and their limited space for storing the large stock of scenery required. In earlier days, when theatres employed a regular troupe of players and when scenery was largely restricted to stock scenes representing The Mall, The Country Inn, The Chamber, The Palace, the task of organizing scenic effects could be performed by the prompter who was also responsible for calling the actors to rehearsal and handing out their parts. These duties he performed under the overall control of the leading actor. We see Quince performing precisely this task with some typical interjections from the leading actor in *A Midsummer Night's Dream*. There were occasions, such as the great court masques and the medieval mystery plays, when a master of the stage was required to co-ordinate the actors, the scenery, the machines, and the effects; but this was not the general practice. Now, with the increasing emphasis upon scenery and lighting, and the need for careful selection of actors from a floating profession, a higher authority than the prompter was required to make the decisions and weld all the elements together.

The Advent of the Director

At first the mechanical tasks were delegated to a stage-manager who relieved the prompter of such responsibilities and who was directly under the control of the actor-manager or the theatre manager, but in time—though not before the end of the century —the leading actor yielded his overall direction of the actors to the producer, later to be called the director. This change of control was gradual. Henry Irving, by super-human effort, managed to act as producer, manager, and leading actor at the same time, but the task killed him. The playwright Tom Robertson, whose plays required greater realism than those of his contemporaries, was the first to advocate the need for a co-ordinating director. Robertson both as playwright and technician was one of the principal predecessors of realism; in *Caste* (1860) the common man emerges as a more lifelike delineation of character.

It was probably the influence of the Saxe-Meiningen Players which eventually persuaded the actors of the superior results to be achieved under independent direction. This company was formed and directed by George, Duke of Saxe-Meiningen in 1874. The Duke was a master of stage-craft, and insisted that scenery should be not merely a decorative and suggestive background, but must serve the actors' movements and provide them with acting areas. He created for the first time a plastic setting by breaking the stage surface into various levels; above all, he was a master of crowd movement. Every member of his crowds was treated as an individual instead of one of a motley collection of 'supers'. There were no 'star' actors and every part was given its due value, whilst great attention was paid to each individual costume whether it was worn by a member of the crowd or by the actor playing the leading role. The Saxe-Meiningen company influenced the future development of the European theatre, not least in London, which it visited in 1861, and in Moscow, where it greatly influenced Stanislavsky. Duke George of Saxe-Meiningen was, in fact, the first stage director.

The direction of the Saxe-Meiningen company was mainly confined to the artistic co-ordination of the physical elements of stage-craft. Greater depth and detail were required in the direction of the realistic plays which from Robertson's *Caste* onwards began to flow into the theatre, and the need for direction was further emphasized by the plays of the French naturalist movement, which, in Zola's phrase, sought to present 'the man of flesh and blood on the stage, taken from reality, scientifically analysed, without one lie'. Antoine in Paris, Stanislavsky in Moscow, and Otto Brahms in Berlin were to discover other aspects of the director's craft—namely, his responsibility for the interpretation of character, the creation of atmosphere and the re-integration of the playwright with the theatre from which he had for so long been divorced.

But the advent of the all-powerful director was brought about by other factors as well as the need for co-ordination and greater attention to realistic detail. The industrial revolution, which had broken down the barriers of society as well as the barriers of communication, had brought about a new liberalism of thought. Society no longer had an accepted vision of life and the theatre was no longer—as it had been since the time of the Greek ritual theatre—an expression of an accepted social outlook. Public taste was fickle; there was no certain guide to the sort of plays that would be acceptable; nor was there an accepted artistic convention for their performance. The theatre was free to choose and this implied a personal choice. To the director, therefore, fell the responsibility of formulating the way in which a play should be interpreted and this led to a variety of directorial cults of a highly individual nature.

The successors of Stanislavsky, Antoine, and Brahms developed increasingly individual and sometimes eccentric characteristics. Meyerhold, Vakhtangov and Tairov, Copeau, Dullin and Baty, Reinhardt, Jessner and Brecht were to find new ways of interpreting the play and to provoke much controversy about the rights and duties of the director who during the last sixty years has been the greatest single influence in fashioning the art of the stage.

In Britain the first stirrings of the director's theatre, following the example set by the Meiningen company under the iron discipline of its royal martinet, had some influence on the actor-managers as they wrestled with painting, music, history, and archaeology in their heroic attempts to provide a homogeneous style. But it was not until the twentieth century was well under way that the director, as an individual, emerged to give a new impetus to the style of acting. The romantic style lingered on occasionally rising to great summits of inspiration when a Beerbohm Tree or a Forbes Robertson commanded the stage, but too often sinking to banality and bathos when lesser fry tried to imitate them.

The tide of romanticism, which came roaring in as a protest against the outworn traditions and artificialities of classicism, was perhaps too violent and too demanding on the actor-managers to last. Although the romantic actors through the power of their personalities were able to maintain their hold over the theatre and subjugate the rather indifferent playwrights whom they employed, the seeds of weakness were visible from the earliest days of the movement. The wild and untamed imagination, escaping from the rules of reason and the discipline of classical style, had no weapons other than its horns with which to fight the devastating ridicule of its intellectual critics. The maddened bull that had rushed head-first into the arena was felled by the thin, cold rapier of George Bernard Shaw. It was not a difficult nor a glorious conquest, for economic as well as artistic reasons brought about its downfall. The force of romanticism was already spent when Irving gallantly fought its cause. Its weakness was its lack of contemporary authors of quality and its enormously costly productions; its real enemy was the gradual improvement in the educational standards of the new mass audiences.

The Naturalistic Theatre

The theatre of naturalism, for which Shaw and the critic

William Archer acted as the British champions, was the inevitable development of the growth of realism which ever since the domestic drama of the 18th century had been a growing factor in the literary expression, as well as in the visual elements, of the theatre. The naturalist theatre started in a small theatre for a minority audience in Paris in 1887. Its first home was a squalid wooden shack which seated 343 spectators; its first leader, André Antoine. Its strength was, first, that it tempted the artist-playwright back into the theatre—here was a theatre in which he was not ashamed to participate. And, secondly, it was a theatre in which the section of society, which did not follow the cult of materialism or the banalities of romanticism, could believe. It was described by Zola as 'a slice of life' and its object was to record actual life on the stage as exactly as possible and without comment. Drama was to follow in the steps of the new men of science—the zoologists, the botanists, the evolutionists—by studying humanity with clinical objectivity. From Paris the new movement spread to Berlin and Scandinavia, but its greatest stage manifestation was the Moscow Art Theatre and its master Konstantin Stanislavsky.

In 1898 Konstanin Sergeivich Stanislavsky formed—jointly with his co-producer, Nemirovich-Danchenko—the Moscow Art Theatre, in which the techniques and philosophy of modern realism and naturalism were developed. Theatricality and stage mannerisms were ruthlessly swept aside, and the actor, together with all the appurtenances of the stage—scenery, furniture, properties, and off-stage noises—were brought as close to life as the limitations of the fundamental artificiality of the stage would allow. This illusion of actuality was aided by the invention of electric light as well as by the development of three-dimensional scenery which took the place of the old flat wings and back-drop. The stage became a solid room from which one wall was removed, and everything that happened within the frame of the picture was as seemingly unconcerned as possible with the presence of spectators. Acting was no longer an idealization of life, it was life with all its vulgarities, its commonplaces, its half-spoken thoughts,

I

its awkward pauses, its meaningless gestures. The romantic theatre strove to paint life larger than it is; its art lay in a certain untamed magnificence. It delighted in portraying abnormalities, rather than normality: madness, violence, and the supernatural; man stretched to the limit of his powers and placed in the most bizarre circumstances. Its staging was lavish, costume plays being preferred to contemporary dress; it delighted in pageantry and elaborate scenery, in painted wings and back-drops, gauzes and transparencies representing a highly coloured representation of nature. Although it sought after historical accuracy, this accuracy was romanticized: a view of the Roman forum was painted to provide the most picturesque aspect; Hamlet's castle was presented with sinister gloom; the bridge over the Rialto was shown bright with gondolas and bathed in sunlight. Romantic acting was broad, sweeping, sometimes frightening, always exaggerated, intensely theatrical. It favoured the burning quality of personality, emphasizing melodramatic pauses, heightened gesture, and facial contortion. Yet, if the art of the naturalistic theatre lay in making the insignificant, significant, in creating drama out of seeming normality, it recognized that no man is normal—for normality is as unreal as the supposition that there is such a thing as 'the ordinary man' or 'the man in the street'. Every man is an individual, masked behind a screen of conventions. Naturalism displayed the conventions, and, by means of them, revealed the individual. No playwright of this objective naturalism equalled Anton Pavlovitch Tchekhov (1860–1904) in accurate observation and sympathetic approach. Perhaps the fact that he was a practising doctor in constant touch with human weakness made it possible for him to remain unbiased and allowed him to paint humanity divorced from political or moral polemics and armed only with pity and gentle humour. This accurate observation of actual behaviour did not prevent him from recording the poetry of life, for to Tchekhov life moves to the harmony of nature, and good and evil, folly and wisdom are all part of a lyrical pattern. This lyrical pattern in which his characters move is recorded, too, in their speech-phrasing and in their silences. Indeed it is often in the silences that the poetry is heard—the distant rumble of a train approaching, the fall of the axe upon the cherry trees, a guitar playing in the distance, or that strange sound 'that seems to come from the sky, like a breaking harpstring, dying away mournfully'. But the harmonies Tchekhov heard during his pauses does not always take audible form and should not be forced to do so. Tchekhov objected strongly to Stanislavsky's desire to fill the pauses with frogs croaking, crickets singing, and clocks ticking, for these silences are the pauses in which the inner reality of character is expressed—they are the soliloquies of naturalism.

Tchekhov recorded life as he saw it, the rich and the poor, the comedy and the tragedy, and for him comedy and tragedy were for ever mixed. We can laugh at the misanthropy of Ivanov and the exaggerated seriousness of Konstantin—and the next moment they have shot themselves. No playwright since Sophocles has possessed such a power to evoke pity or has made, without polemics, such a case for human mercy. But his plays are full of irony; he himself labelled them as comedies, and they have been much misinterpreted in our theatre by a tendency to play them too seriously. The reasons for the failure of his plays in this country at the turn of the century are not difficult to understand; the portrayal of human life contained in them is neither tragic nor comic, neither melodramatic nor sensational; they demand a delicacy of playing and a team of experienced actors of equal merit to play them, and above all the co-ordination of a director to balance their subtle ingredients and to bring out their flavour. Such conditions did not exist in the London commercial theatre at the turn of the century. As a result, his finest plays—*The Seagull* (1896), *Uncle Vanya* (1899), *Three Sisters* (1901), and *The Cherry Orchard* (1904) were seen or understood by a small section of the community and their influence in British theatre was only felt many years later.

Meanwhile, in Stockholm August Strindberg (1849–1912) was creating his own naturalistic theatre. At the Intima Teatern many of our modern stage devices and machinery, such as revolving and sliding stages, were devised and lighting techniques were improved. As a playwright Strindberg was more adventurous and more inventive than Shaw or Tchekhov. His style embraced naturalism in *The Father, Easter,* and *Miss Julie,* as well as surrealism in *The Dream Play,* a play which was far in advance of his time. His plays are characterized by a deeply rooted hatred of women, which led him to depict a distorted and often tortured view of life.

In Berlin Otto Brahm founded Die Freie Buhne in 1889; a theatre modelled on Antoine's Théâtre Libre where the repertoire was almost exclusively devoted to the plays of the new naturalistic school. Its greatest achievement was the discovery and production of the plays of Gerhart Hauptmann (1862–1946), whose *Vor Sonnenaufgang* (1899), *Einsame Menschen* (1891), and *Die Weber* (1892) displayed his sympathy for down-trodden humanity and his careful observation of character. Hauptmann later turned to fantasy; a tendency which is found in many of the naturalist playwrights including Strindberg, Shaw, and O'Casey, but although *Die Versunkene Glocke* and *Hannele's Himmelfahrt* are still played on the German stage, he never again reached the heights of his realistic masterpiece, *Die Weber.*

The naturalistic playwright, like the scientific observer, explored and recorded the phenomena of nature—the ugly as well as the beautiful, the conscious mind as well as the sub-conscious, the reason as well as the imagination—and these he brought together in circumstances as natural as possible, without recourse to a heavily-scored dramatic plot. And yet these elements are, by the art of their selection and the inner conflicts which develop from them, highly dramatic material. There is nothing more dramatic than Strindberg's *The Father,* and not even the dying words of Hamlet can draw more tears to our eyes than the last words of Firs in *The Cherry Orchard*:

Life has slipped by as if I'd never lived. I'll lie down. There's no strength in you, nothing left for you—all gone! Ah, you . . . good for nothing!

Naturalism in the hands of such artists as Tchekhov, Strindberg and Hauptmann brings together the reason and the imagination in a harmony that we can claim to be a true art.

Social Drama

The new movement to ally the theatre more closely with living people was finally brought to its logical conclusion by allying it with social issues. The master builders of the realistic theatre were the two giant playwrights, Henrik Ibsen (1828–1906) and George Bernard Shaw (1856–1950). Neither can be called an objective observer of life, for both were imbued with an aggressive desire to comment on it. If the naturalistic writer as explained by Zola can be compared with the late nineteenth-century man of science, recording as faithfully as possible the anatomy of the human mind and the peculiarities of man's behaviour, then Ibsen and Shaw may be compared with the late nineteenth-century non-conformist preachers who delighted in mounting their pulpits and tearing the masks off seemingly respectable society. In fact Ibsen, Shaw, Strindberg and Hauptmann were all part of the revolt against the hypocrisy and false social values of materialism, a revolt that was to culminate in revolutions both bloody and bloodless in every country in which materialism flourished. The masks that the new dramatists tore off society were not only the evils of society, but its misplaced virtues. Idealism which fails to recognise humanitarian realities, morality which clings to conformity, sentimentality which cloaks sexual relationships, and the false position of woman in society were the targets that attracted Ibsen and Shaw. Neither can be called an innovator of stage techniques; for, in fact, the play forms they used were in the main based on the well-made play of the bourgeois theatre, though, like all the realists, they occasionally sought relief by painting on a larger canvas. And whilst Ibsen often used poetry and symbolism, Shaw used a prose which in its rhythms and balanced phrases often reminds us of the Restoration stage language. But, whilst both were concerned with plays whose subject matter treated the living social issues of their time, there is a considerable difference in their attitudes to the purpose of the theatre. Ibsen was primarily an artist, Shaw primarily a critic. For this reason Ibsen provided the best acting parts, Shaw the better situations. Ibsen's characters live in their own right, whereas Shaw's are often the mouthpiece of the playwright.

The poet in Ibsen is seen not only in his major poetic dramas such as *Brand* and *Peer Gynt*, nor only in the symbolism of *The Lady from the Sea* and *The Wild Duck*, but no less in the use of atmosphere and mood which pervades the realism of his heavily upholstered parlours with their windows curtained with lace against the pale Northern sun. This use of atmosphere to create a climate in which drama takes place was, in fact, a new development in theatre made possible by the realism of stage techniques. No director or designer of an Ibsen play can afford to neglect it, for atmosphere in Ibsen is a character in the drama, no less important than the ritual of Greek tragedy, the poetic action of Shakespeare and the lyrical patterns of Tchekhov. This atmosphere is closely bound up with the architecture, costume and furniture of the late Victorian epoch and the director must, therefore, follow closely the fashion and taste of that epoch in his contemporary production. It is impossible to divorce plays like *Ghosts*, *Rosmersholm*, *A Doll's House*, and *Hedda Gabler* from historical taste, it is, however, possible to create the atmospheric influences by modern techniques such as lighting and greater realism of scenery than Ibsen's stage could provide. But in the performance of Ibsen we should not be reaching for archaism, but for the deeper realism of atmosphere. In Ibsen's plays three-quarters of the plot has taken place before the play begins; what happens to the characters is the result of what has happened before the curtain rises. These ghosts of the past which lurk in the corners of the over-decorated interiors—the Captain Alvings, the Mrs. Rosmers, the little Eyolfs, as well as the past mistakes, the frustrations, the selfish idealisms and the veiled truths—cannot be hidden if the true reality of the plays is to be found. They pervade the plays, living again in the lives of the characters, in the furniture, the books, the dusty photograph in the corner, the oil-lamp and the shadows it throws on the wall. This atmosphere is the poetry of Ibsen, it is the poetry that Dylan Thomas creates, it is, in fact, the poetry of realism.

Shaw was no poet, but a superb rhetorician and an incorrigible jester. The calibre of his genius was tougher than Ibsen's. For him there were no mysterious ghosts of the past, his plays are brilliantly lit with the hard, cold light of reason. His characters are not involved in the expiation of their sins, but in the tough struggle with a life-force around which there is no mystery or atmosphere.

No one knows better than Shaw how to handle an audience; for his place was in the hustings engaged in the lively art of persuasion, in which his sense of the ridiculous and his endearing habit of turning the tables on himself endowed his plays with a superb sense of light entertainment whilst driving home the toughest argument. Yet despite the laughs which Shaw offers to his actors, the roles he created are less satisfying to play than the grim creations of Ibsen. Ibsen's characters take possession of the actor and live inside him; Shaw was incapable of allowing such freedom to his characters; they are the creation of his brain and the expression of it. To interpret Shaw's characters we can gain little from our own inventive powers—that is perhaps why Irving, who was pre-eminently an intuitive and creative artist, refused to play them; the main values will be found in a mastery of Shaw's phrasing, of knowing where to place the emphasis and how to manage the tempo. Even the movement and gestures provided by the stage-directions are unyielding to the actor's personal approach. Shaw was fundamentally incapable of giving himself to the theatre or indeed of giving himself to anything other than himself. His essay on Ibsen, *The Quintessence of Ibsenism*, turned out to be the quintessence of Shavianism; and his *Black Girl in Search of God* was really in search of Shaw.

But plays that aimed at the mind of the audience found little appreciation from Victorian and Edwardian society. During his life-time Ibsen's plays were never able to spread much further than the little playhouses and the art theatres of London, however popular they may have been in other lands.

The London dramatic critics greeted *Ghosts* with invective that has hardly been equalled in the history of the theatre. 'This mass of vulgarity, egotism, coarseness and absurdity.' 'A piece to bring the stage into disrepute and dishonour with every right-thinking man and woman.' 'As foul and filthy a concoction as has ever been allowed to disgrace the boards of an English theatre.' Such was the reception with which so-called intelligent critics greeted the greatest playwright since Shakespeare.

Shaw fared little better in America, where *Mrs. Warren's Profession* was hounded by attacks so virulent that they make the critics of Ibsen seem mild in comparison. In London Shaw was merely regarded as a mad revolutionary whose plays were to be avoided by decent citizens.

It was largely due to the pioneering work of the producer, Harley Granville Barker, and the support of the critic, William Archer, that a home was found in which a small public could enjoy or be scandalised by the plays of Ibsen, Shaw and the early social dramatists. But Shaw was a brilliant propagandist; no-one knew better how to woo the public to the new school of playwriting. With greater cunning than Ibsen and endowed with a native sense of humour and mischief which Ibsen lacked, Shaw eventually found a larger public with *Pygmalion, St. Joan, Arms and the Man,* and *Candida,* and by forcing open the doors of the larger theatres to his own plays he created a public for all social drama.

The British playwrights were not slow to adapt the new styles of social playwriting to suit the needs of a predominantly middle-class society. Arthur Wing Pinero (1855–1934) and Henry Arthur Jones (1851–1929) provided a more popular, if less crusading form of social drama, which made no violent assault on the public's conscience and deprived social realism of much of its essence by removing its sting. As Shaw pointed out, Pinero and Jones had a tendency to run away at the last minute from the problems they had raised. Neither Pinero's *The Second Mrs. Tanqueray* nor Jones's *Mrs. Dane's Defence* could be calculated to do more than raise eyebrows in late Victorian and Edwardian drawing-rooms.

CHAPTER FOURTEEN

THE CONFUSION OF STYLES

THE THEATRE OF THE EARLY TWENTIETH CENTURY

THE concluding years of the nineteenth century and the opening of the twentieth saw a confusion of stage styles and techniques stretching from the romantic acting of Irving and Beerbohm Tree to the new naturalism of Stanislavsky. In London the predominant style was characterized by the idealized realism, or drawing-room acting, of George Alexander and Gerald du Maurier, which placed greater reliance on technique than on analysis of character. Against the exaggerations of the romantics and the artificial behaviour of the drawing-room performers two voices cried out for a return to the elemental ritual of the theatre. Neither Craig nor Appia were able to achieve the sort of theatre they advocated, but both were prophets of the stage of our own day, and in their scenic art, at least, have influenced our outlook and techniques.

Edward Gordon Craig, born in 1872, was the son of Irving's leading lady, Ellen Terry, and at one time a member of Irving's company. Despite his difference of outlook from that of his master, Craig has always preserved an ardent admiration for Irving, recognizing in him the same passionate devotion to theatre as an art as he himself possessed—a passion that he found totally lacking in the shopkeeping mentality of the West End theatre. Craig's practical work as a director of plays was hardly seen at all in England and only on a few occasions on the Continent. His influence was mainly exerted through *The Mask*, a journal that he edited from his self-imposed exile in Florence, and through his book *On the Art of the Theatre*.[1] In these publications

[1] Heinemann, 1911.

he exhibited his woodcuts of costumes and scenic designs which are noble and evocative, but to state that Craig was an impractical scenic designer is not a fair assessment of his contribution to the theatre; it is unhappily a view that has been cultivated by the commercial managers who rejected him. Unpractical he was, and many of his theories, such as his call for a theatre of super-marionettes instead of actors, are over-stated, but his refusal to accept a theatre which had become the slave to out-of-date conventions and dominated by actors more interested in their billing than their art was in itself a powerful contribution, coming at a time when the popular British theatre had sunk low in performance and outlook. His vast three-dimensional screens, which bear little relation to the actual dimensions of Victorian and Edwardian stages, his utter disregard of the problems of moving and masking them, his suggested use of light to emphasize the sculptural form of his scenic arrangements may have been beyond the technical equipment of the theatres of his day, but they opened the door to a new vision of theatre which was eventually to lead to the revolt against the scenery of photographic illusion and to the replacement of the interior decorator by the scenic artist. Both Yeats and Max Reinhardt were inspired by him and in America Lee Simonson and Norman Bel-Geddes found ways of transforming his dreams into actualities.

The Swiss designer and theoretician Adolphe Appia (1862–1928) was inspired by the Wagnerian ideal of theatre as a composite work of art (*Gesamtkunstwerk*), which fused together the various arts of its component parts into an art in its own right. Dialogue and acting, he argued, could not fully express what he called 'the hidden life' of a play; this 'hidden life' must be expressed in the complete integration of scenery, movement, music and especially the lighting. Appia's designs, like Craig's, are non-representational, making use of proportion, space, and varying levels to bring about the rhythmic movement of the actors.

But, whilst the aesthetics of Craig and Appia found expression in the German and eventually in the American theatre they had no effect on the fashionable theatres of London, where the only form of scenic art consisted in the skill with which the stage-carpenter, the painter, and the interior decorator could make the stage look as real as possible and at the same time satisfy the taste of the public for the display of luxury and ostentation.

Drawing-room Plays, Realism, and Fantasy

Amongst the plays that found favour with fashionable audiences at the turn of the century there emerged one brilliant satire of the absurdities of bourgeois snobbishness and fashionable materialism. Oscar Wilde's comedy *The Importance of being Earnest* (1895) revived the best traditions of the Restoration artificial comedy and remains one of the masterpieces of the British theatre. Wilde's other comedies, *Lady Windermere's Fan*, *An Ideal Husband*, and *A Woman of No Importance*, though never lacking in wit, are marred by the regard he paid to the sentimental and melodramatic conventions of his age. Pinero was no less affected by current fashionable taste in his well-made plays with their contrived curtains and melodramatic situations, but he displayed a ready humour and a fine sense of the ridiculous in his farces, *Dandy Dick* and *The Magistrate*, which are, perhaps, the most enduring of his plays.

Drawing-room plays, like the plays of the Restoration, are seen at their best in comedy. Somerset Maugham following the path of Wilde enlivened the stage at the opening of the present century with comedies of sophistication and wit. *Lady Frederick* (1907), *Caroline* (1916), and *Our Betters* (1917) are amongst the best examples of this narrow and artificial play form, a form which unhappily became a formula to be followed by too many playwrights lacking the wit of Wilde and Maugham.

The deeper realism of ideas, which had proved unpopular in the form served up by Ibsen, was, however, turned out in a more acceptable form when mixed with fantasy and humour, and Shaw pursued his policy of irritating and amusing the public, providing a repertoire of brilliant, argumentative drama which was to find an international audience. Indeed Shaw has often been more popular abroad than he has in England; partly because the British public has never quite adopted reason as a major ingredient of drama, and partly because, whilst a predominantly middle-class audience likes to laugh at the foibles of the aristocracy and the quaint vulgarities of the lower classes, it has never been quite so happy at laughing at itself. John Galsworthy (1867–1933) and Harley Granville Barker (1877–1946) followed in the path of Ibsen and wrote social plays like *Strife* and *Waste*, which were deeper in content and less timid than Pinero's, but lacked Ibsen's poetic atmosphere and Shaw's humour and eloquence. Sir James Barrie (1860–1937) in plays like *Dear Brutus, Mary Rose, The Admirable Crichton*, and *What Every Woman Knows* combined realism, charm, fantasy and sentiment with the craftsmanship of the well-made play.

 This tendency to mix fantasy—sometimes disguised as symbolism—with naturalism was noticeable in many of the plays of the older realists. Ibsen found that actuality, even when endowed with a social purpose, was an insufficient medium of his dramatic expression. Some form of poetic expression has always been a necessary ingredient in drama. Tchekhov found it in poetic mood, Shaw in extravaganzas, such as *Back to Methuselah*, or by placing his plays of ideas in remote or antique civilizations, Ibsen in the poetry and symbolism of *Peer Gynt* and *Brand* or in the heavily charged, fatalistic atmosphere of his later plays. This movement away from naturalism was pursued by the Belgian playwright, Maurice Maeterlinck (1862–1949), whose plays *The Blue Bird, The Betrothal, The Burgomaster of Stilemonde*, and *Pelleas and Melisande* won considerable popularity in London. In them Maeterlinck mixed reality with an unseen and mysterious power which controls man's destiny. His characters often appear as messengers from another world, surrounded by the misty symbolism of *Art Nouveau*. Meanwhile in Ireland a great poet turned his hand to the theatre. The plays of W. B. Yeats are perhaps too strictly poetic and mystic to take their place in the popular theatre, for, whilst Yeats forced himself to master the technique of the theatre, he lacked the instinct of a dramatist and made great demands on the imagination and poetic appreciation of his public. In his early plays, *Land of Heart's Desire* (1894), *The Countess Cathleen* (1899), and *Shadowy Waters*, he appealed to the newly awakened spirit of Irish nationalism. Thereafter—except in *Cathleen ni Houlihan* (1902)—he moved away from urgent issues and sought new theatrical forms by exploring the possibilities of mythology and legend, in such plays as *On Baile's Strand* (1904) and *Deidre* (1906), and the traditions of the Japanese Nō plays in *Four Plays for Dancers*. In many ways his plays complement the visual approach of Gordon Craig, who designed a set of screens and costumes for them; both Yeats and Craig demanded the highest artistic approach to the theatre and a return to the simplicity and severity of Athenian and medieval ritual. Yeats's influence, though not widely spread, was considerable. Poet-dramatists of the present century such as Gordon Bottomley, T. S. Eliot, Christopher Fry, and Bertolt Brecht owe much to his outlook and inspiration.

But neither the purism of Yeats nor the cataclysm of the First World War did anything to shake the basic materialism of British theatre managements. The London theatre became a fairground for the huge influx of troops seeking relaxation and oblivion from the horrors of trench warfare, and neither poetic drama nor plays of ideas—if they contained any serious thought—could find a large public. *Chu Chin Chow* presided supreme over a crazy dance of death. Much of this fairground atmosphere remained in the West End theatre after the war ended; indeed London, as a great tourist centre, has never quite recovered its theatrical individuality; its major theatres no longer cater for a predominantly local public. Like Broadway, the West End theatre has become a place for the entertainment of visitors.

The post–1918 theatre saw the development of musical comedy, whilst farce and detective plays provided distraction for the shattered mentality of a society anxious at all costs to patch up the fearful chasm which had been revealed in the midst of its structure. The plays of ideas returned, but only slowly did they make their way back, avoiding serious issues and heavily submerged beneath the artificial life of drawing-room comedy. Naturalistic techniques were combined with the lightest possible theatrical fare. The stage was made as solid and real as possible. The one-set play was favoured, not only because a drawing-room or a court scene could be more solidly constructed if left un-disturbed by scene-changes, but also because the cost of labour and materials, together with the many other enhanced costs of post-war theatre, made it imperative to exercise rigid economy. Competition, too, was now keener; the cinema, with its greater facility for realism and spectacle and its considerably greater economic potential, was a dangerous rival in attracting the public; many who went to the theatre for light entertainment were drawn away to this easier and cheaper amusement. The days of the romantic spectacular drama were over; spectacle was more convincing on the screen than on the stage. Playwrights were encouraged to write little plays, plays with as few characters as possible, dressed in modern dress, and confined to one room. Only in musical comedy, where managers could be more sure of attracting a large public, did lavish spectacle continue.

Among the playwrights of the drawing-room John Van Druten in *After All* (1929), *There's Always Juliet* (1931), and his study of adolescence, *Young Woodley* (1928), gained equal popularity with Somerset Maugham's accomplished and neatly turned comedies, *The Circle* (1921), *The Letter* (1927), and *The Constant Wife* (1927). Frederick Lonsdale following in the wake of Maugham wrote such popular successes as *The Last of Mrs. Cheyney* (1925), *Spring Cleaning* (1923), and *On Approval* (1927), and provided the books for popular musical comedies. But perhaps the most accomplished of the drawing-room dramatists is Noël Coward, who both as composer, actor, dramatist, and writer of revues, dominated the theatre of the nineteen-twenties and thirties. In his early plays, *The Young Idea* (1921), *The Vortex* (1924), and *Fallen Angels* (1925), Coward was regarded as the spokesman of his generation, expressing much of the disillusion-ment and the desire to escape of the 'twenties. Later he turned to romantic sentiment and sentimental patriotism in *Bitter Sweet* and *Cavalcade*; and later still in the 'thirties and 'forties to witty satire in *Design for Living* (1932), *Blithe Spirit* (1941), and *Present Laughter* (1942). His more recent work has proved less popular, for the escape he offers from current anxieties is no longer relevant or practicable, but he stands beside Terence Rattigan as a rallying

The Big House (1926) show his firm adherence to the well-made play tradition, but also a sympathetic understanding of the political and patriotic aspirations of his country. Inspired by the ideals of Irish nationalism, a new naturalism was born, which found its highest expression in Sean O'Casey. *Juno and the Paycock* (1924) and *The Plough and the Stars* (1926) are amongst the greatest masterpieces of naturalistic drama. But like other naturalists O'Casey was dissatisfied with the photographic technique which prevented him from probing deeply enough into human motive, and from expressing his strongly felt political and social views. In *The Silver Tassie* (1928), he introduced elements of symbolism into an impressive war scene in the second act, injecting a greater degree of social comment than he had displayed in his earlier plays. From 1928 onwards his plays have been increasingly concerned with political and social satire employing expressionist techniques.

In Birmingham Sir Barry Jackson's Birmingham Repertory Theatre provided an international fare; as well as introducing new plays, such as John Drinkwater's *Abraham Lincoln* and Shaw's *Back to Methuselah*. At the Maddermarket Theatre in Norwich, Nugent Monck continued the experiments of William Poel, who in the early years of the century had rediscovered the Shakespearian stage, presenting Shakespeare's plays not only in the Elizabethan dress of their time, but upon an unlocalized stage and without scene divisions. Monck's actors were local amateurs, and the life he created around his theatre was in many ways a more true expression of regional culture than those repertory theatres which, except for the Dublin theatres, recruited their actors and producers from the London stage. At the Liverpool Repertory William Armstrong and Basil Dean created a centre of good acting and a high standard of professional production. In Glasgow a theatre for Scotland was born, which produced at least one international dramatist in James Bridie.

But the greatest manifestation of theatre outside London was, and still is, the Stratford-upon-Avon Memorial Theatre (now the Royal Shakespeare Theatre) which has become a Mecca for Shakespeare enthusiasts and tourists from all over the world.

This, however, can hardly be considered as a part of the repertory theatre movement.

Meanwhile, another development was taking place outside London which was to add to the prestige of the British theatre and provide an opportunity for theatre enthusiasts to see good theatre and to meet and discuss its art. This was the introduction of the dramatic festival pioneered by Sir Barry Jackson at Malvern in the nineteen-thirties, where an annual festival presented four hundred years of drama commencing with revivals of the old religious plays and progressing forward through the ages to new plays by Bridie and Shaw. At the Canterbury Festival, Eliot's great poetic tragedy *Murder in the Cathedral* (1935) was first seen and so were several of the plays of Christopher Fry. More recently the York Festival of religious drama, the festivals at Edinburgh, Pitlochry, Chichester and Bath, as well as other centres, have added much to the dramatic life of the century.

The Little Theatres

In London the conception of the small art theatre was introduced by the Vedrenne-Barker management at the Royal Court Theatre (1904–7) where many of the plays of Shaw and Ibsen were presented. At the Mercury Theatre under the management of the playwright and theatre enthusiast, Ashley Dukes, a new interest in poetic plays was developed. The plays of W. H. Auden, Christopher Isherwood, and Ronald Duncan sowed the seeds of a literary tradition which was to reap a rich harvest when eventually the plays of T. S. Eliot and Christopher Fry reached the West End. At the Gate Theatre, the Westminster, the Arts, the Little, and the Embassy experimental and continental plays were first performed, and at the Lyric Theatre, Hammersmith, the old Restoration comedies were given a brilliant revival under the management of Sir Nigel Playfair.

All these streams fed the river of British theatre in the first three decades of the twentieth century, and it was largely owing to the influence of these often uneconomic ventures that the West End theatre recovered from its fevered war-time atmosphere of frivolity and gradually returned to more serious plays.

CHAPTER FIFTEEN

THE NEW CONTINENTAL AND AMERICAN THEATRE

The New Continental Theatre

WHILST Britain had been able to gloss over the cracks created by the First World War in the structure of its society, Germany and Russia had not. In these countries changes of a fundamental nature had occurred which brought their pre-war theatre to the ground and swept their ruling classes, their accepted establishments, and seemingly unshakeable ideas in the dustbin. In Russia the old Imperial Theatres were taken over in the name of the Soviet people; in Germany the Court Theatres were transferred to the city and state governments. The revolutions which both countries underwent were reflected in their style of acting, production, and playwriting. In Russia, Meyerhold and Tairov broke away from the naturalism of Stanislavsky; in Germany, Erwin Piscator and Bertolt Brecht assaulted the theatre on all sides of its orthodox conventions and outlook. It would be useless in a short survey to explain and illustrate all the theories that arose in the 1920's and 1930's in these two countries. It was an age of 'isms'—expressionism, dadaism, futurism, cubism, constructivism, sur-realism—all of which were attempting to find an alternative to the strongly entrenched orthodox naturalism. Almost every new experiment was hailed as a new theory and was the reason for a new manifesto on the art and purpose of theatre. Meyerhold, the most radical of the Soviet producers, endeavoured to mechanize his actors, turning them into the super-marionettes that Craig had suggested; texts were projected on a screen above the stage, the front curtain was swept aside, the cyclorama dispensed with, the bare brick wall of the theatre was exposed, and a wooden construction used in the place of scenery. The film was employed as a moving background to the actors by Piscator and Brecht, as well as lantern slides representing caricatures or rough sketches of the scenery. Every effort was made to divorce the stage from any illusion of reality. By every means in their power the new dramatists, and more especially the new directors, strove to remind the spectator that he was not observing real life, but taking part in a theatrical performance. In Max Reinhardt's production of Georg Büchner's *Danton's Death*, actors were scattered amongst the audience whilst songs were introduced by Brecht and others to break the continuity of emotional involvement by the audience. The techniques of the Chinese Classical Theatre and of the Japanese Nō plays were studied, which divorced acting from reality, and in which the actor was not emotionally involved in the character he presented. The theatre aimed at achieving a dispassionate approach, forcing the spectator to think for himself and not allowing him to be lulled into acceptance by identification of himself with the actor, but urging him instead to identify himself with the social or political meaning of the play. But, if the spectator was asked to think for himself, the new theorists were determined that the outcome of his thought should be positive. For Meyerhold, Brecht and Piscator, the purpose of theatre was political, and the new theatre of the 'isms' became in fact a didactic theatre which assaulted the stronghold of naturalism.

Meanwhile, Pirandello in Italy was discovering a new type of play in which the actor stepped out of his character and observed the play from the outside, analysing the motives and criticizing the acting of the characters themselves. *Six characters in Search of an Author* (1921) has had a profound influence on breaking down the conventions of the naturalistic theatre.

More important, however, than Pirandello's revolt against the conventions of the well-made play was his revolt against the philosophy of social establishment and his disruptive view of the hopelessness of man's reliance on reason or faith. For Pirandello there was no truth, since every man held a different view of truth, whilst communication between individuals had no meaning since words cannot express so many interpretations of truth. In his final play, *Henry IV*, sanity itself has no meaning, since it is devoid of a standard by which it can be judged. The pessimism and unbelief of Pirandello profoundly influenced many post-war European playwrights; more particularly are its effects seen in the existentialist plays which followed the Second World War.

In France the revolutionary theatre of Russia and Germany made little impact. The French theatre has always been more sensitive to the values of evolution than the theatre of other European countries; its flow has been more continuous, and its traditions, in consequence, have the power of a living force, rather than hardening into out-moded conventions. Whilst the Comédie-Française represents a conservative element, its offspring have used its basic traditions to evolve new styles, which are rather new ways of revealing the essential truths of those traditions than revolts against them. The civilizing influence that emanated from France after the First World War was represented by its artist-directors no less than by its playwrights. In line of descent from Antoine's naturalism, came Georges Pitoëff and Lugné-Poë. The former presented many of the plays of the new writers, such as Claudel, Cocteau, and Anouilh, as well as the works of foreign dramatists. More than any other French director Pitoëff was responsible for creating a new interest in Shakespeare by providing productions which were less encumbered with romanticism, and more in keeping with contemporary French taste. Lugné-Poë, also encouraged the new dramatists of the post-war period. At the Théâtre de l'Œuvre he was responsible for introducing the works of Maurice Maeterlinck and Claudel's *L'Annonce faite à Marie*. At the Théâtre Montparnasse, Gaston Baty brought scenic art and lighting to a state of naturalistic perfection which has seldom been equalled. His décor, which was often better than the plays he presented, was distinguished by its taste and atmosphere of authenticity. Scenic design, too, was studied by Jacques Copeau, the greatest of the French masters of the new stage-craft. At Le Vieux Colombier, Copeau's study of stage-craft led him away from the naturalism of Antoine and Baty towards symbolism. For him each object on the stage should have a meaning, and that meaning should be an expression of the play. This led to a general simplification of the scenery and of its nature and purpose. The three-dimensional scenery of Baty with its atmospheric, but naturalistic, lighting was replaced by the stylistic 'object' of Copeau, selected and placed, often on a bare platform, so as to tell its own tale without distraction and with functional purpose. From Copeau came many of the new actors and directors, including Louis Jouvet, Charles Dullin, and Michel St. Denis. His company of young actors, La Compagnie des Quinze, which was responsible for producing the plays of André Obey, *Noë* and *Le Viol de Lucrèce*, had a profound effect on the British stage when it visited London shortly before the Second World War.

In Russia, Maxim Gorky (1868–1936) spans the gulf between the old naturalism of Tchekhov and the new political ideas of the revolutionary theatre. His first great play, *The Lower Depths*, was performed in 1902 and his last plays, *Yegor Bulichev* and *Dostigayer*, in 1934; Gorky remained faithful to naturalism, whilst embracing the didactic sympathies of the Bolshevist stage. The Russian experimental theatre was short-lived, for it was not long before the new mass audience of the Russian proletariat revolted against the complicted intellectual theories that Meyerhold and Tairov had evolved in the belief that they were serving a people's theatre. A rigid definition of the purpose of Communist art was imposed, and the theatre was dutifully led back to the safe confines of realism. The only remnant of the new outlook that remained in the reformed Soviet theatre was the didactic or propagandist slant. This political purpose of theatre grafted on to the naturalistic technique of the Stanislavsky system became the basis of what is called Socialist Realism: a term which implies that all art must be conformist in political outlook, as well as understandable to majority audiences. The German reformers, too, were hurried away from their obscure theories by the Soviet reforms, for most of the German innovators were Communist sympathizers who could not afford to stray too far from the decrees of Moscow. The Nazi régime finally scattered the German progressives and killed, for a time at any rate, the anti-naturalistic movement of the German theatre. Only one great experimental theorist remained from this wild revolution against naturalism, Bertolt Brecht, whose plays—*Mother Courage and her Children, The Life of Galileo, The Good Woman of Setzuan,* and *The Caucasian Chalk Circle,* have assured him a lasting place in dramatic literature.

The American Theatre

Meanwhile, in the 1930's a new theatrical force of considerable power was beginning to influence the British and continental theatre. The history of the American theatre may be said to have started when the first professional company of actors arrived from Britain. This was in the 1750's when Lewis Hallam and his company set up a 'stock' theatre in Williamsburg. There were many interruptions and hurdles to be overcome before the American theatre could settle down to a healthy national development—not least the necessity to overcome the colonial outlook of the audience. The history of the American theatre during its early years followed closely on the lines of development in Britain. It was, in fact, an extension of the British provincial theatre, performing much the same repertoire as the 'stock' companies in the English cities. In the early nineteenth century signs of a national drama began to emerge, but such plays as *The Indian Princess* (1820) by James Nelson Barker, *Octoroon* by Dion Boucicault, and *Our American Cousin,* were based upon the romantic traditions of the spectacular London melodrama.

As wealth increased, so theatres sprang up in greater numbers in New York; and from 1869 onwards when Augustin Daly built Daly's Theatre, the increase in number and magnificence of the playhouses in New York quickly made it the theatrical centre of America and one of the richest theatrical cities in the world.

Large theatres and spectacular productions brought an increased emphasis on romantic acting, as they had done in England. American actor-managers, like Edwin Forrest (1860–72), Junius Brutus Booth (1821–83), Edwin Booth (1833–93,) and William Gillette (1855–1937) staged the same sort of repertoire—the familiar mixture of Shakespeare and melodrama —as their colleagues in London. The improvements in trans-Atlantic communication brought many of the great British and continental actors to New York, and these visits were reciprocated. As American actors began to win fame overseas they inevitably increased their prestige at home, and so the 'star' system developed, as it had done in London, and the actor-managers and the 'long-run' plays drove the old 'stock' companies out of business.

The rise of a successful commercial theatre brought about a gradual process of monopoly which in turn drove out the actor-managers and placed control of the Broadway theatres in the hands of business-men, who had little interest in the artistic values of the stage, and less in encouraging a native drama, unless it could be shown to be profitable. But the national consciousness, which had been growing throughout the latter half of the nineteenth century, was inevitably destined to show itself in the theatre. From 1915 onwards, when the Washington Square Players (later to become the Theatre Guild) were founded, American drama began to win a hearing from the public. Among the pioneers of an American theatre were the Provincetown Players, who from 1920 onwards began to present the plays of Eugene O'Neill. *The Emperor Jones* (1920), *The Hairy Ape* (1922), *The Great God Brown* (1926), *Strange Interlude* (1928), *Mourning becomes Electra* (1931), brought world recognition to the American theatre. Other art theatres such as the Neighbourhood Playhouse and Eva le Galienne's Civic Repertory took a firm stand against the commercialism of Broadway, and with their assistance playwrights such as Sidney Howard, Robert Sherwood, Elmer Rice, and Maxwell Anderson began to break down the 'show business' prejudice against serious American theatre. Their productions were enriched by the work of such outstanding scenic-artists as Norman Bel-Geddes, Lee Simonson, and Robert Edmond Jones who had been strongly influenced by the designs of Gordon Craig and the staging of the great German director, Max Reinhardt.

From 1930 onwards the new American drama was firmly established on Broadway and such plays as Maxwell Anderson's *Winterset* (1935), Marc Connolly's *Green Pastures* (1934),

Lillian Hellman's *Little Foxes* (1935), John Steinbeck's *Of Mice and Men* (1937), and Clifford Odet's *Golden Boy* (1937), were successfully challenging the less vigorous plays of the British dramatists on their home ground.

Contemporary Influences from Europe and America

The Second World War brought in its wake a mood of pessimism which is symbolized by the existentialist plays of Sartre, the 'absurd' plays of Eugene Ionesco, and the abstract symbolism of Samuel Beckett. Beckett's play, *Waiting for Godot*, and the plays of Ionesco have had a more immediate effect on British writing since the Second World War than any other plays except the works of Bertolt Brecht. For many they have come to symbolize the final break-away from naturalism and the conventions of the 'well-made' play.

Besides Brecht, only two writers in the German language Friedrich Dürrenmatt and Max Frisch, have achieved an international reputation since the Second World War. Both are, in fact, Swiss, and both are writers of comedy.

Dürrenmatt in a lecture entitled *Problems of the Theatre* has explained that today tragedy has no meaning, since tragedies are now carried out by giant machines. 'Hitler and Stalin', he argues, 'cannot be converted into a Wallenstein.' Tragedy pre-supposes an ordered universe; but, since the world is changing in a revolutionary way, he maintains it can only be reflected through comedy. To a great extent his attitude is shared by many contemporary writers in the French and British theatres, and much of the comedy that has emerged from the new writers leans heavily towards the grotesque, the symbolical, and the satirical. There is a superabundance of ideas that seem to fall over each other in an anarchic and inconsequential way; there is laughter, but no gaiety.

From the contemporary Italian theatre the plays of Diego Fabbri and Ugo Betti have been widely presented outside their native country. Ugo Betti's play, *The Queen and the Rebels*, has achieved a success in Britain, which is due in no small measure to Betti's ability to reflect the prevailing mood of pessimism without losing confidence in the essential nobility of human beings.

French theatre is rich in dramatists, embracing such divergent styles as the surrealism of Jean Cocteau, the existentialism of Salacrou and Jean Paul Sartre, the religious plays of Henri Ghéon, the muscular Catholicism of Henri de Montherlant, the gentle and analytical plays of Jean-Jacques Bernard, the abstract symbolism of Genêt, and the comedy-satires of Jean Anouilh. The latter playwright has had a greater success with contemporary British audiences than almost any playwright—continental or British—of post-war years. His style embraces comedy, fantasy, melodrama, and tragedy in such widely different plays as *Ring Round the Moon, Thieves' Carnival, Antigone, Traveller without Luggage, The Lark*, and *Becket*. As with Betti his success is due to his ability to tell a dramatic story and reflect the anxieties and doubts of the present combined with a faith in the dignity and greatness of human beings. This combination is found in a more intellectual form in the plays of Henri de Montherlant.

Amongst American dramatists who have brought new lustre to the American stage and new ideas to international theatre since the Second World War, Arthur Miller and Tennessee Williams have opened the way to a more poetic form of naturalism. In *All My Sons, Death of a Salesman,* and *The Crucible,* Miller has avoided the mood of impotent despair which has swept over so many of the contemporary plays of the Continent and has now reached our shores. Whilst recognizing man as the victim of society, Miller has shown him to be the creator of the conditions in which he lives. In the last resort, as in *The Crucible*, man can by his will and, if necessary, by his own sacrifice, contribute to redressing the evil he has created.

The plays of Tennessee Williams with their mixture of common reality and poetic conventions have won a popular audience, which is, perhaps, more due to their sensational situations than to their enduring qualities. His poetic conventions, which are expressed in the form of narrators, symbolism, and such expressionistic media as projections on a screen or the dream-like treatment of *Camino Real*, are often his least successful attempts to break away from naturalism, but his true values lie in his penetration of the deeper truths of human behaviour, more

especially the behaviour of neurotic humanity, and his ability to
create atmosphere which at its best is invested with much the
same poetic quality as Tchekhov possessed.

Whilst Broadway has opened its doors to a certain type of
American play, its economic structure allows little opportunity
for home-grown experiment of a radical nature. And, whilst
foreign plays which take an unusual or imaginative approach may
be welcomed as novelties, the same hospitality is not shown by
Broadway audiences to American plays which break away violently from the conventions of the well-made play. To some extent
the off-Broadway theatre provides a home for the unusual, and,
indeed, the success of Jack Gelber's dramatized documentary,
The Connection, and of Edward Albee's excursions into abstract
symbolism in *The American Dream* and *The Death of Bessie Smith*
would have been impossible in the highly materialistic conditions
of New York's West-End. But the American Theatre suffers from
the very considerable gulf between the highly successful and the
complete failure. Whilst the university theatres and the few
repertory theatres may be able to offer some opportunities to the
playwright whose plays are not likely to achieve immediate
success on Broadway, the financial inducements that they, or the
off-Broadway theatre, can offer are insufficient to compensate for
failure to reach the accepted national market.

It is significant that in a world of divided ideologies the most
powerful theatre emanates from those who, in one form or another,
have been able to retain their faith in man. This faith may be
represented by the political convictions of Brecht or the religious
beliefs of de Montherlant and T. S. Eliot, whose plays *The Master of
Santiago* and *Murder in the Cathedral* must rank amongst the masterpieces of western theatre, or it can be represented by the intense
humanism of Arthur Miller. A mood of pessimism may be largely
true of the age in which we live, and to disregard that mood would
be untrue to life which the theatre must reflect, but to disregard
the potential nobility of man or to despair of his ability to sur-
mount the evils that he has created, is to deny the very founda-
tions of his existence. Pessimism, whilst it has its time and place
in contemporary theatre, is not an enduring human theme.

CHAPTER SIXTEEN

REVOLUTION IN THE THEATRE

BRITISH THEATRE TODAY

THE Second World War, unlike the first, brought a stimulus to theatre in Britain. Whereas the theatrical fare during the 1914 War had been almost exclusively light entertainment, during the 1939 War interest in more serious theatre, particularly in ballet and the Classics, was stimulated and spread throughout the country. Much of the credit for this was due to the creation of the semi-governmental organization, at first called the Council for the Encouragement of Music and the Arts (C.E.M.A.) and later the Arts Council of Great Britain. The creation of the Arts Council marks a significant change in the official attitude towards the arts generally and to the theatre in particular. No longer is the theatre regarded as the concern of private enterprise alone. With the development of the Welfare State intelligent use of leisure becomes a matter of public responsibility, and the theatre takes its place as an asset of no less importance than recreation facilities and libraries. Without the assistance provided by the State through the Arts Council the theatre might well have sunk under the weight of its wartime problems, and almost certainly would have emerged weakened and curtailed during the difficult years of readjustment which followed it. But without the general desire of a wide section of the public that the theatre should be preserved from the ruin of war and the restrictions and shortages of its aftermath, the meagre funds at the disposal of the Arts Council would have been inadequate to keep it alive.

This change in attitude was brought about partly by the nature of the war itself which, because of the greater disruption of civilian life, induced a deeper realization of the issues at stake than had the fevered atmosphere of death and patriotism in the muddy desolation of Flanders. No longer did society believe that the end of the war would produce a return to the life of the past. The whole economic structure of the country was crumbling, and there was an urgent search for new ideas and a new way of life. Imagination was released from the confines of reason, since reason could no longer deal with the effects of the atom bomb. In the search for an answer to the problems, both economic and social, which were raised by the complete destruction of the philosophy of materialistic security, the theatre, through its playwrights, became a valuable medium of expression. Britain's intense isolation was broken down together with its belief in self-sufficiency, and the influence of new theatrical thought both from America and the continent began to be felt. The plays of Arthur Miller as well as Tennessee Williams brought new ideas of social realism from America, whilst from Paris the plays of Jean Anouilh and Sartre reflected the insecurity and anxiety of post-war society. The London stage became increasingly cosmopolitan: foreign companies from Paris, Italy, Moscow, East Berlin and China brought with them new techniques to influence the outworn conventions of the well-made play.

Amongst the British playwrights who spanned the period of the Second World War and its after-effects there were many who sought by new techniques to express the revolution that was taking place in society. Although widely different in approach such considerable playwrights as J. B. Priestley, T. S. Eliot, Peter Ustinov, Christopher Fry, and James Bridie experimented with time plays, poetic drama, the use of imagery, extravaganza, symbolism, and religious ritual to meet the needs of an audience that was increasingly dissatisfied with the escapist drama, detective plays, and the drawing-room dramas. Priestley in *Time and the Conways, I Have Been Here Before, Johnson over Jordan,* and *They came to a City* has done much to break down the prejudice of the public against the 'unusual' play, whilst Eliot and Fry have paved the way for the acceptance of poetic drama. But the social revolution was deeper than the form of the play itself; it concerned a total change in the theatre: a change in the architectural form of theatre, in its scenic art, in its acting, management, and direction. The old conception of theatre as a cultural decoration was dead; so, too, was the conception of theatre as the entertainment of an exclusive leisured class. The end of the war was the beginning of a social revolution that has not yet ended. This revolution has deep spiritual as well as economic and social significance; it demands from the theatre a corresponding revolution in its outlook.

To meet the needs of the new theatre a form of management is being evolved which is no longer primarily concerned with making profits for distribution to its backers or shareholders. The management of the new theatre often takes the form of a non-profit-distributing Trust, supported by the State or the City Council, or both, which pays back its profits into the theatre itself. It seeks to provide a balanced repertoire of plays with at least some shape or policy in their selection. So far as possible the new managements try to keep together their team of actors, directors and designers and develop them into a co-ordinated ensemble, having their own workshops and their own audience organizations. Managements like the Old Vic, the Royal Shakespeare Theatre (at the Aldwych Theatre and at Stratford-on-Avon) the English Stage Company, Theatre Workshop and the larger repertory companies may well prove the pattern for the theatre of the future.

The old figure of the theatre manager as a 'boss' with the power to make or break his casual stage-labourers, strutting into the rehearsals with his cigar and the traditional gardenia in his button-hole to make awe-inspiring comments on the way a scene should be played or an actress should be dressed, or undressed, is disappearing. Dwindling profits resulting from competition from other sources, combined with higher costs are hastening his departure. And finally his bluff is being called by the actors, who now realize that he no longer knows what the public wants and have at last dared to claim back the theatre as their own.

The nature of the director, too, has changed or developed. Whilst much of the responsibility of management has fallen on his shoulders, such as the choice of play and the casting of it, the new director has ceased to be the martinet, shouting his instructions at the actors from the back of the stalls. He is now the leader of a team of fellow artists, and his authority is based on the respect his abilities can command. The old maestro whose word was law, and who only communicated as much of his thoughts about the meaning or intention of a play as were necessary to make the actors do what he wanted, has given place to the colleague of the actors, who discusses his views frankly with his actors, and is ready to adapt them to suit their particular capabilities.

The actors, too, have changed. The influence of Stanislavsky and Brecht has developed a new seriousness in the outlook of the actor and a wider and deeper consciousness of his relationship to his profession as a whole, as well as to society. The actor no longer sees himself as a pampered star or a casual labourer with no responsibilities beyond his own performance on the stage. He is no longer prepared to shelter behind the glamourized personality built up for him by the purveyors of publicity, he is concerned with the relationship of theatre art with other arts, with politics, with social attitudes and with the building of audiences, and he is not afraid to speak his mind and to accept sacrifices to achieve what he believes to be right. John Osborne's picture of the old actor's attitude in *The Entertainer* is not without significance in the new actor's attitude towards the revolution in the theatre.

The change in the actor's attitude to his relations with society has been accompanied by a change in his style of acting. The influence of Stanislavsky's analytical approach to the creation of character with its emphasis on realism has been re-inforced by the greater realistic requirements of television. Television acting demands a naturalism of speech and behaviour suitable for a small audience gathered round the television screen in the living-room. This new acting style—if style can be said to apply to acting which is devoid of artifice—can result in inaudibility and failure to convey meaning in the theatre where a muttered remark and the slight twitch of an eyebrow cannot be brought into the sharp focus of the close-up. To some extent actuality, as opposed to theatricality, has been encouraged by the techniques of the documentary film. This type of social documentary programme, which started as a film recording actual life and has been developed by the radio and the television into a documentary play performed by actors, demands an absolute naturalism of speech and behaviour. The audience is required to believe that what it sees and hears is actually taking place; any hint of theatricality will, therefore, result in a suspension of belief. As a result, not only have many actors become accustomed to perform in actual, instead of theatrical, terms, but the new audience, nurtured on television, has come to expect this form of expression.

The new emphasis on naturalism in performance is a radical, though not a logical development of Stanislavsky's method. Stanislavsky taught the actor to seek the truth of the character he was acting in terms of motivation, but he did not advocate the abandonment of theatrical means to convey the truth. For him truth meant theatrical truth; the interpretation of the truth of the spoken word in movement, expression and gesture by theatrical means, which implies by means that are immediately significant to a theatre audience. The new naturalistic acting has reduced the theatrical means to a minimum with results that are often destructive to the essential nature of theatre. Whilst actuality is beneficial in that it has destroyed many of the clichés that develop around theatricality, it is destructive when it denies the existence and validity of theatrical expression. Its extreme practice may be valid for the social documentary, either in the mechanical theatre, or in such stage forms as *The Connection* and *The Apple*, but it is not a true form of interpretation for plays that are neither written nor conceived in terms of actuality.

The Well-made Play

The most significant force in the revolution in the theatre is the new form of playwriting. When establishments wobble and class structures fall, when nuclear discoveries and the mysteries of space create wide cracks in the surface of reason, when man no longer needs to be reminded of his guilt of which he is only too painfully aware, when anxieties gnaw holes in the placid surface of existence, then imagination breaks out in nightmare distortions

9. 'A superb architectural concoction . . .'
A stage setting by Giuseppi Galli (Bibiena Family).

10. The Fore-stage and its doors.
The Dorset Garden Theatre (1671).

of reality. The well-made plays are no longer an expression of a way of life, for life, itself, appears to have no plan.

Before we dismiss the well-made play, the name of which dates back to the first half of the nineteenth century, though the form can be traced back to the age of reason, we must examine what is meant by it.

Briefly the well-made play embodies a philosophy and a structure. The philosophy has changed from age to age, the structure had not radically altered.

During the first seventy years of the nineteenth century the philosophy was the embodiment of the materialist outlook: the preservation of the ethical, social and political structure of society.

Pinero and Henry Arthur Jones undermined this philosophy, not so much by direct attack upon it, since society was not ready for radical change, but by examples of where it fell down. *The Second Mrs. Tanqueray* shows a 'fallen woman' who conceals her past life and marries into respectable society; she is eventually exposed and in order to save her husband from social ostracism, she commits suicide. Pinero infers that society is wrong in imposing its rigid rules of right and wrong, but he is careful not to stress his moral too strongly and relies on sentiment, rather than reason.

Ibsen, Shaw, Galsworthy and Granville Barker attacked the philosophy more directly. Shaw often took the basic situations of the well-made play's philosophy and turned it upside down. In *Pygmalion* he shows how the poor girl, Eliza, makes nonsense of society's pretensions and flouts the dramatic conventions by refusing to marry her benefactor. In the same way he ridiculed military idealism in *Arms and the Man*, the solid respectability of the clergy in *Candida*, and parental authority in *You Never Can Tell*. Ibsen and Galsworthy attacked with heavier weapons than Shaw's light rapier. Ibsen exposed the hypocrisy of the self-righteous leaders of public opinion, and Galsworthy emphasized the rights of the common man. But whilst these early social realists discarded the philosophy of Victorian materialism, they did not discard the structural form of the well-made play. This form

L

demanded a unity of style and a progressive development of the plot, and the plot itself was a solid piece of dramatic story-telling —the plays had what is called 'a good story-line'. The plot was usually divided into four acts, sometimes into three; the first act was a statement of the dramatic theme, the second and third brought about the development and climax of this theme, and the last the resolution of it. Each act ended dramatically, either with a significant curtain line or with a humorous one. The end of the play was the conclusion of the story, though not necessarily the resolution of the particular social problem which the playwright had set out to present. The play might have a happy ending in a reconciliation or the successful conclusion of a romance, or it might have an unhappy ending in death and desertion; but, whatever the conclusion might be, the spectator was made to feel that this was the right and only way in which the play could end. Love problems, in particular the eternal triangle of two men and one woman, or two women and one man, were an almost inevitable formula no matter whether the play treated politics, religion, murder or industrial disputes. There was often a sub-plot as well as the main plot; the former was expected to be of a lighter nature than the main plot and to act as relief to the latter. Both plots were inter-connected and resolved at the same time.

Scenically the plays were realistically presented, the locations most favoured were the Drawing Room, the Library, the Office, the Court Room. Stage directions were liberally inserted by the playwright; and these often described not only the scenery and the furniture, but the costume and facial expression of the actors. It was clear that the whole conception of the play had been most carefully thought out by the playwright. A well-made play was a skilful and meticulous piece of craftsmanship.

Craftsmanship, too, was evident in the management of dialogue. Economy was a virtue, irrelevant remarks were avoided and the action or characterization were forwarded by almost every sentence that was spoken. Shaw often transgressed these rules, but when he did so it was done with a sense of mischief, rather than as an innovation. Fundamentally he respected craftsmanship and the structure of his plays remained traditional. Noël Coward, Terence Rattigan, James Bridie, and J. B. Priestley preserved the traditional structure, though the philosophic content of their plays was widely different. Although fantasy was used by Bridie, and Priestley often leaves his audience guessing as to whether the action he presents is real or not, we are left in no doubt about what the plays of these playwrights mean and what their plots are about. Whether they adhere to all the rules or not, they accept the general principles of what constitutes dramatic construction.

The New Playwrights

The sudden eruption of a new generation of British playwrights coincided with three major events in the British Theatre, which took place in 1955 and 1956—the productions of *Waiting for Godot* at the Arts Theatre and of *Look Back in Anger* at the Royal Court and the visit of the Berliner Ensemble bringing the plays of Bertolt Brecht to the Palace Theatre. These events, so widely different in character and coming from three different theatrical cultures, are largely emblematic of the main streams of contemporary play-writing.

The approach made by Samuel Beckett in *Waiting for Godot*, which is reflected in the French theatre by the plays of Eugene Ionesco and Genêt, symbolizes the chaotic state of existence by a corresponding anarchy in the construction of the play itself. Play architecture, as it was understood by the writer of the well-made play, has given place to a seemingly abstract void in which plot, or dramatic story-telling, is almost non-existent, characterization is conceived in terms of human symbols, rather than human beings with a past behind them and a future before them, and whilst they appear human enough in the situation in which they are placed, we are not aware of their existence outside that situation. Language is often nonsensical or inconsequential, as if the issues of the play were incapable of being communicated in the terms of coherent dialogue. The exponents of this abstract form of play-writing often achieve a powerful form of sub-conscious communication the effect of which upon the audience can provide a disturbing experience of penetration into a world which is vaguely familiar, but from which we emerge without complete understanding. In consequence involvement with the action of the play is often incomplete and spasmodic. At its best our involvement is hypnotic. In *Waiting for Godot* we are transfixed in a nightmare stage of absorbtion, in which swirling emotions, vaguely recognizable, appear to reveal truths below the surface of the common reality of what is happening on the stage.

This continental school of sub-conscious drama would seem to be in direct descent from the experiments of Strindberg in *The Dream Play* and the surrealism of Jean Cocteau. In Britain this tradition did not exist in the theatre, and, in consequence, experiments in this form are more closely related to our naturalistic roots. The plays of Harold Pinter, such as *The Dumb Waiter*, *The Birthday Party*, and *The Caretaker*, reveal some of the characteristics of the continental school, as do the plays of the American playwright, Edward Albee, but abstraction is less pronounced, and, whilst symbolism is preserved, greater humanity is revealed. In the plays of N. F. Simpson with their satirical overtones, their absurd situations and their largely nonsensical dialogue the relationship seems closer to the absurdity of Lewis Carroll than to the sinister atmosphere of Strindberg.

The approach of John Osborne in *Look Back in Anger* is the approach of the majority of the new playwrights. Here there is a closer affinity with the naturalist tradition than in the plays of Pinter and Simpson. Alun Owen, Shelagh Delaney, Arnold Wesker, Willis Hall, and to some extent Robert Bolt and John Arden are amongst those who follow the naturalist tradition. However, these new naturalists can only be regarded as a loosely related group by no means exclusively devoted to naturalistic techniques. Sometimes, as in Shelagh Delaney's play *A Taste of Honey* or in Osborne's *The Entertainer*, there is a mixture of naturalism with the techniques of the music-hall. Sometimes the playwrights swing decidedly to the epic techniques of Brecht. The plays of the new naturalists, however, share a common attitude in their revolt against the well-made plays as epitomized in the plays of Terence Rattigan and Noël Coward, both in their search for new milieux outside the conventional middle-class background and in their rejection of literary or theatrical language. Their revolt against the well-made play form is seen, too, in their rejection of 'slick' and neat craftsmanship. The architecture of the play in Aristotelian terms of a beginning, a middle and an end is discarded in favour of 'a slice of life' which has no definite borders. But a more radical revolt, and one that is shared by nearly all contemporary playwrights, is their attitude towards the hero or principal protagonist of the action. The jaundiced Jimmy Porter is not only unheroic, but is made deliberately repellent. Even Luther is denied heroic stature, and is shown as an angry man whose revolt against the Church is more due to chronic constipation than to religious conviction. The same detachment in a less strident form is seen in the funny, bewildered characters of *A Taste of Honey*, the unyielding toughness of Sergeant Musgrave in John Arden's *Sergeant Musgrave's Dance*, and in the satirical view taken of his characters by the Irish playwright, Brendan Behan, in *The Hostage*.

This deliberate alienation of sympathy from the protagonists is seen more clearly in the plays of Bertolt Brecht, but there is a difference between the use of alienation in Brecht's plays and in the plays of the British playwrights. For Brecht alienation is used in order that the meaning and philosophy of the play can be judged calmly and without the intervention of sentiment or of theatrical sympathy. But the plays have a meaning and a purpose and these are hopeful and positive. For him the world is 'out of joint', but it can be put right; humanity is bad, but it can be saved. British plays, which have been inspired by Brecht, have followed the epic form without discovering a purpose, other than the purposeless drift towards chaos. For them 'the world is out of joint', but they were not 'born to set it right'. Humanity is satirized sometimes with scorn, sometimes with anger and sometimes with laughter, but only rarely with any indication of man's saving graces. This narrow view of humanity, which so many playwrights feel impelled to take, leaves a feeling of incompleteness in the audience's mind, as if only half the truth were being told.

Amongst the playwrights who share this feeling of helplessness beneath the shadow of the bomb, Arnold Wesker and Robert Bolt have not succumbed to the mood of pessimism. In his intensely human trilogy, *Chicken Soup with Barley, Roots,* and *I'm Talking of Jerusalem,* Wesker displays a love of humanity and an attachment to his characters coupled with a sense of purpose as a playwright. To some extent his political sympathies, despite the destruction of his political allegiance, have provided him with a faith which seems lacking in most of his contemporaries of the new left, but to a greater extent this pity and sympathy for humanity arise from his warm Jewish background with its centre in the family.

Robert Bolt, too, stands apart as a playwright who has a faith in the ultimate values of human ethics. In *A Man for all Seasons* he shows the same belief in the rightness of man's fight for his conscience, as Brecht shows in *Galileo.*

In their search for new milieux in which drama can take place the new generation of British playwrights have successfully broken down the class barriers of the British theatre in much the same way as Clifford Odets and Arthur Miller had done for American Theatre a generation earlier. But the 'kitchen sink' label, which has been unfairly attached to them, is by no means the end of the road. The new dramatists have found that they can express themselves in wider fields than the narrow drawing-room drama could do, and against backgrounds as far removed as Luther's Germany, Moore's England, the fictional provincial town of the mid-nineteenth century in *Sergeant Musgrave's Dance,* the Irish 'Troubles' of *The Hostage,* and the jungle patrol of *The Long and the Short and the Tall* by Willis Hall.

If they have not found a philosophy of life, they have at least illuminated the problems and anxieties of our age; more than that we can scarcely ask of them, until life itself finds a new faith and meaning.

The New Stage

The breakdown of play construction is reflected in the architecture and scenery of the contemporary theatre. Theatre architecture of the pre-war years was, as we have seen, a logical development of the theatre of illusion as it was introduced from France and Italy by Killigrew and Davenant in 1660. Its features are well known to us and were required by the plays and society it served. First, the separation of auditorium and stage by the proscenium arch with its heavy velvet curtain was eminently suited to the neat act divisions of the well-made play. Secondly, the division of the auditorium into sections was devised for the accommodation of a class-conscious society. Thirdly, the raised stage surmounted by a tower housing the grid, for raising and lowering the scenery, was required by the convention of scenic illusion. The whole arrangement was not only right for the structure of society, but also for the structure of the plays. There has been very little new building in Britain to illustrate new techniques; these are seen at their best in the new theatres of Scandinavia, Germany, and in the American universities, where radical ideas of adaptable staging are being developed. In general the new theatres comprise a complete reorganization of the auditorium, so as to provide equal opportunities for all to see and hear the play, with price differences reduced to a minimum, together with a flexible stage, capable of being transformed into a variety of shapes and sizes, which can house the illusionary stage, the 'apron' stage and even such extreme forms as theatre in the round. At the Mermaid Theatre in London the proscenium arch has been totally removed and the stage area treated as a continuation of the auditorium. In the new theatre at Chichester and in the theatre at Stratford, Ontario, an adaptation of the Elizabethan stage, combined with the semicircular Greek auditorium, has been adopted.

In many of the new theatres the means of providing scenic illusion in the form of the box-setting and the painted backcloth have been abandoned, and a return to the principles of the space stage of the Greek and Elizabethan theatres encouraged. But the fixed stage, whether it be in the older illusionary form or in the open platform style, presents problems for the playhouse, that has to cater for a repertoire of plays of all styles. The answer would seem to be a flexible stage which can change its shape to suit the play.

Clearly the degree of illusion supplied by the scenery must depend on the style of the play, but in the contemporary theatre irrelevant decoration is as much out of place as it is in industrial design. The skilful use of lighting and the use of architectural structure in the place of painted illusion are the general aim of the scenic designer. But above all he aims at providing a functional form for the action, rather than decorating it. The scenery is no longer required to be beautiful for its own sake, and the round of applause that greeted it when the curtain was raised is seldom heard in the modern theatre.

Revolution in the Theatre

A revolution in the British theatre was long overdue, for the theatre was not only out of step with other arts, but it was out of step with the theatre of other lands. To a great extent the revolution was made possible by the weakening of the profitable potential of the theatre. Once show-business became no business the way was open for *The Other Theatre*—to borrow Norman Marshall's title[1]—to move in. The commercial manager who had not already fled to more profitable fields was at least willing to allow the rebels to try their hands at a trade in which he was clearly at sea. In an effort to create a vital theatre allied to modern thought and geared to the needs of a new society the rebels struck wildly at every convention associated with the materialist theatre of the past.

The rational approach, the craftsmanship of the well-made play, the middle-class milieu, the use of pictorial scenery, the proscenium arch, even the Aristotelian theories, were assaulted regardless of merit on the grounds of past associations.

Any revolution which is bottled up for long is bound to explode in a drastic form. It may be that much of contemporary playwriting is intolerant and many of the new actors are lacking in appreciation of the stylistic demands of the stage, but these are temporary symptoms. In time the enduring values of the past will be discovered and used, as the past must be used, to bring new life to the theatre of the future.

[1] Lehmann, 1947.

CHAPTER SEVENTEEN

CREATIVE INTERPRETATION

THE SEARCH FOR A PHILOSOPHY

IN the course of our journey through the past some of the problems of staging old plays for a modern audience have been mentioned, but clearly the problems are more complex than these brief notes have revealed.

Many books have been written on the history of the theatre, but few on the living performance of that history. The pressures of theatrical production seldom allow the stage-artist leisure to reflect on the guiding principles of what should be the relationship between the past play and the contemporary audience and what his rights and duties are in relating the one to the other.

Despite the need to please and entertain the theatre must have a philosophy of its own. Whilst 'we, who live to please, must please to live' may be the ultimate role of theatre, there remains the question: what are the boundaries of the pleasure we seek to provide? We call dramatic theatre 'the legitimate stage'. What does 'legitimate' mean in terms of dramatic performance?

The Philosophy of Theatre

The philosophy of the stage is usually studied in terms of contemporary taste or technique: the new fashion of playwriting and the new system of acting, directing, or designing. The principles which should govern the new techniques in relation to plays of the past and the rights and duties of the stage-artist as the interpreter of past plays are vaguely covered by such negative expressions as 'taking undue liberties', 'not a legitimate action', or 'going too far'. The responsibility of the stage-artist to the living author is reasonably clear, but in the case of the dead author this responsibility is loosened and the personal taste of the stage-artist, coupled with a wholesome fear of making 'the judicious grieve', provides both the boundaries and principles of legitimate interpretation.

It is in the study of the relationship of the past to the present, and of what the stage-artist should be doing when he relates the one to the other, that the philosophy of theatre can be most fruitfully developed; for in this aspect of theatre we have to consider not only the actor-audience relationship as it exists today, but as it existed in the past. This study will lead us to a wider view of theatre than a study of contemporary techniques of performance can provide and raises the question of what we mean by interpretation in a deeper and more complex form. It will not tell us how to write plays, act, design the scenery or make up our faces, but it will open up vistas of theatre wider than a study of current taste or methods. For lack of a philosophy we think in terms of what is currently fashionable and are bound by a hit-or-miss attitude; we are unable to judge or criticize justly since we have no yardsticks of what is legitimate. What we need is a philosophy which searches the reality or truth of interpretation. The most significant contribution to this philosophy of theatre today comes from the socialist-realists whose study of performance techniques is based on the teaching system of Stanislavsky, but whose theory of creative interpretation of past plays requires that the philosophy and meaning of those plays should be related to Marxist doctrine. There is nothing radically new in this view of the function of creative interpretation. When the Restoration actors revived the plays of Shakespeare they twisted or slanted their philosophy to suit the political and social views of their own age.

In a liberal society we have no need to use the theatre to spread political views nor to justify social conduct; nor can we legitimately consider the alteration or slanting of a play's philosophy or outlook to be creative interpretation. A limitation on the stage-artist's creative freedom does not restrict his freedom to interpret the play in terms of his personal taste and by means of his

personal technique. But taste and technique concern the act of interpretation—the way in which we interpret—not the action we
propose to interpret. The act of interpretation is legitimately conceived in contemporary terms; we do not require nor wish to see an
archaic reproduction, but we do require the stage-artist to enrich
our experience by interpreting the philosophy or meaning of the
play truthfully, not altered to conform to our well-worn ideologies.

Truth in theatrical terms requires that the action of the play
be presented in a manner that makes us believe it is true; this we
call verisimilitude. It is, therefore, necessary that the philosophy
and meaning of the play be conveyed to us in a manner that we
can believe in, but it is not our duty nor our right to alter or
adapt the philosophy or meaning in order to provide verisimilitude.

Creative Interpretation

To translate or interpret a play of the past in terms of verisimilitude, whilst preserving the truth of its philosophy or
meaning, is one of the hardest tasks that confronts the stage-
artist. Taste changes from age to age and what seemed right to a
small boy watching his first pantomime might well seem wrong if
he were to see it twenty years later. Frequent change in taste is
more common in western countries than it is in the East, where
taste can take on a dual character, and both the old and the new
taste can exist side by side.

In Japan a performance of a Kabuki play in a manner dating
back to the early seventeenth century is as acceptable a form of
verisimilitude as a modern production in the western manner.
In western countries, where traditional methods have not the
same vitality or appeal, an old play is only acceptable if its
technique of performance conforms to the current taste.

The art of the theatre is more sensitive to the changefulness
of taste than the art of the painter, sculptor, poet, or composer,
for it makes use of a medium which either reflects or controls
taste; this medium is the living interpretation of the actor,
director, and designer.

When we look at a primitive painting of the Crucifixion we accept the taste of the painter. The lack of perspective, the gold sky, the plates stuck on the heads of the principal characters represent a medieval taste preserved in time, like a fly in amber. There is no living element to come between us and the medieval conception of this event or action. But when we see the performance of a medieval play of the Crucifixion the action of the medieval source is interpreted to us by the actor. The actor cannot reproduce; being an artist he must create, but the process of interpretation is not pure creative art, in the sense that the dramatic poet can claim to be the creative artist of the play he writes—it is Creative Interpretation; as such it is subject to disciplines which to some extent must determine its liberties. Whilst the Japanese actor of Kabuki makes use of traditional techniques, handing down his ancient skills of movement, gesture, and speech patterns from generation to generation, he still does not claim to give an exact reproduction of his predecessor's skill. There is always a creative element in the actor's art.

Our western habit of theatre is further removed from traditional techniques than that of the Far East and permits greater liberties of creation. The western actor, aided or guided by the director and designer, interprets the action afresh by means of his creative powers and skills in the light of the given circumstances of contemporary taste. The greater the stage-artist, the less dependent he will be on the accepted taste and the more liberty he will exercise in creation. The great stage-artist in the western theatre is he who creates taste and by his art persuades his audience that his interpretation is reality. This liberty to create taste, which is not permissible to the Kabuki actor, is a liberty which places upon the stage-artist a considerable measure of responsibility to the original style of the play; this responsibility is often forgotten or deliberately disregarded. What then are the responsibilities of creative interpretation and what disciplines can be applied to this art?

The Responsibilities of Creative Interpretation

In the theatre we cannot go back in time and see a play

through the eyes of a past generation. If we were able to return to the theatre of Sophocles, Shakespeare, or Goethe, we would be shocked by much of what we saw and indeed many of the conventions of the past would make it impossible for us to see the eternal values contained in the plays. We would not share the religious mysteries which surrounded the performances of a Greek play, nor applaud the blood and thunder of the Elizabethan playhouse, nor revel in the passionate romanticism of the early nineteenth century. The scenery, the costumes, the behaviour and speech of the actors, and, indeed, the behaviour of the audience, would be strange to us, perhaps even ludicrous.

We are forced, therefore, to renew the past, to build a bridge between the past and the present. This bridge must be built by creating a harmonious alliance between the play as it was and the play as it must now be. The essence of this process is to achieve a harmony between the two halves of the bridge. The stage-artist is not justified in using the play merely as a vehicle for the display of his own talents—such was the way of many an actor in the past; it is still the way of many a director in the present. Nor yet is it the function of the stage-artist to twist the purpose or philosophy of the play so as to give it a social, moral, or political slant which suits the mood of the times—such is the way of socialist-realism. What principles, then, should he adopt?

First, we can recognize that a degree of alienation from a play can be an advantage. It is easier to understand a situation, if we see it in retrospect, than if we stand too close to it. Thus a play which contains a situation or problem of eternal dramatic interest does not necessarily reveal the full significance of that problem or situation by being presented to us in the speech and surroundings of our everyday life. The alienation of time provides a greater reality and a greater universality; it allows the play to work its way to our reason through the use of our imagination; it allows us to grasp a truth which is often deeper than a contemporary statement of that truth can be.

It is not, therefore, necessarily an advantage to dress Hamlet in modern dress, to provide him with a revolver instead of a sword. Modernization does not of itself increase our understanding of

Hamlet's problem nor ally that problem to our own lives. It can have the effect of reducing the significance of the eternal truths contained in the problem by robbing them of the authority which time gives to old things. The only advantage in playing an old play in contemporary costume is to release it from a too rigid convention which threatens to stifle its vitality. Some of the productions of Shakespeare in modern dress which occurred in the nineteen-twenties had a valuable shock effect at a time when the playing of Shakespeare had become dangerously static; when identification between the audience and the playwright had lost its fresh impact. If we are, therefore, to preserve a degree of alienation, the problem we face is to find a way of bringing the past forward into the present, and this demands a full under-standing of the past and of the present; for the essence of the problem that confronts us is how to ally age and youth; how to put old wine into new bottles without destroying its flavour. It is a difficult and delicate task, and it is obviously no answer to revert to the past and to recreate all the period peculiarities of the original performance. But there are aspects of the past which we must incorporate in our modern production if we are to bring the past forward with its important values intact. It is a question of selection and adaptation, of being able to marry the necessary peculiarities of old stagecraft to the style of contemporary performance. Let us turn to Shakespeare's stagecraft to illustrate this.

First, the question of the female characters. We know that boys acted the women's parts in Shakespeare. Today we have no boy actors really capable of playing these parts and, even if we had, a contemporary audience would not accept this traditional technique except as a novelty or 'gimmick'. Secondly, there is the question of Shakespeare's unlocalized stage. The fact that Shakespeare's theatre possessed no machinery to change the scenes and no artificial lighting to turn day into night imposed upon the playwright and his audience the acceptance of certain conventions and techniques of stagecraft, some of which are alien to our conception of theatre today, but one of which—the absence of pictorial scenery—is an essential feature of the style of his plays. Today we have grown accustomed to some form of scenic representation and to the technical advantages of electric light, and if we play Shakespeare in an open yard by daylight we shall not be bringing the past forward into the present, we shall be putting the present back into the past. Yet if we ignore the convention of the unlocalized stage we rob the plays of essential qualities; for the unlocalized stage, as we have seen, allowed the dramatist to preserve continuity of action so that event could follow on event without raising the problems of time or place; more important still, it brought about a greater use of the audience's imagination by using words—in fact, poetry—instead of a visual image to create theatrical effect.

Here, then, is an aspect from the past that is of the utmost value to the performance of the play in the present. It is a convention which until comparatively recently was overlooked by those who were concerned in making Shakespeare's plays suit the taste of later audiences.

Style

The task of the stage-artist is to convey the meaning and philosophy of the text in such a way that identification between the text and the audience is established, and the key to the problem lies in the interpretation of the style of the original and the reconciliation of the main aspects of this style with the main aspects of the taste of our own age.

Michel St. Denis, one of the foremost exponents of style in the theatre, has summarized the problems of style in his book, *Theatre, the Rediscovery of Style*:[1]

The theatre's means of expression are forged by the time in which a play is written and performed, and by the contribution of the past. In each country the theatre addresses itself to the public of its time which in due course will become a 'period'. Each period has its own style even though we are not conscious of it as we live it.

The written text of a play is the product of two forms of style: there is the style of the playwright *and* the style of his period.

[1] Heinemann, 1960.

By the playwright's style we mean the way he writes; the language he uses; the imagery he employs; his feeling for character, situation, and atmosphere. If we read or see Shakespeare's plays fairly frequently we have no great difficulty in knowing his style of writing. We can distinguish a passage by Shakespeare from a passage by Congreve; whilst we may not be scholars, we know the difference between his early style and his later style; we have a fair idea of the differences between his lines and those of his collaborators in plays like *Pericles* and *Henry VIII*; we know the sort of characters he creates and the way in which he develops his situations.

Next to the style of the playwright there is the style of the period in which the play was written, by this we mean the outlook and way of life of the period. These factors—the playwright's style and the style of his period—condition in a general way the philosophy and content of a play and in a particular way the dramatic form in which it is written.

Since the playwright's style is inviolate in our definition of creative interpretation, nothing would seem to be easier than to lift the play out of its period style and set it down in our contemporary playhouse, divorced from all the considerations of its origin, time and place. That is precisely what the Restoration actors tried to do, and in doing so they found the plays as written by Shakespeare did not fit their stages, nor suit the taste of their public. They were forced to rewrite, either wholly like Dryden in *All For Love*, or to alter the text like Nahum Tate.

In the nineteenth century an attempt was made to take the period with the play, but the actor-managers mistook the meaning of period. Charles Kean, Irving, and Tree tried to improve upon the Elizabethans' ignorance of antique periods by dressing Shakespeare's historical plays in what passed for genuine historical costume. They failed to see that these plays belonged to the period in which they were written, not to the period in which their action was supposed to take place; that *Julius Caesar* is concerned with Rome as the Elizabethans saw it, not Rome as a nineteenth-century audience saw it. To impose a new antique style on Shakespeare is destructive both to the playwright's style

11. The Actor-Manager's Theatre.
Charles Kean's production of *Macbeth* (1853).

12. The Open Stage.
a The theatre at Stratford, Ontario.

b The National Theatre, Mannheim (Kleines Haus).

and to that of his period, and neither the spectacular scenery of the nineteenth century nor their embattled armies provided a stylistic equivalent to Shakespeare's style.

The discovery of the reality of the style of the period allows us to penetrate more deeply into the truth of the past than does archaeological or historical research. The factor that the stage artists of the past overlooked is that the playwright's style is closely interwoven with the period style. So that if we try to lift the play out of its period style and place it in contemporary style without regard to its period, it is like trying to transplant a flower without its roots.

William Poel at the turn of the nineteenth century began to throw light upon the problem of Shakespearian production when he presented the Elizabethan Stage Society in costumes of Shakespeare's times upon a platform stage arranged in what was at that time believed to be an Elizabethan manner. But Poel's productions, whilst they freed Shakespeare's style from the cumbersome trappings of the nineteenth century, tended to be archaic and ignored the wider issues of creative interpretation.

The discovery of a play's style is achieved by a deep penetration into the feeling of a play and its period. Stanislavsky quotes the poet, Pushkin, as saying:

The truth of passion, the verisimilitude of feeling, placed in the given circumstances, that is what our reason demands of a writer or a dramatic poet.

This applies no less to the stage-artist. His feeling for a play must be a reality; not only must he have a passionate desire to convey the meaning of the play to an audience, he must also be able to convey its feeling, and this feeling is its style. But this style must be allied to the given circumstances of the age in which he lives—to the taste of his audience.

A feeling for style—which is a sub-conscious reaction— is an essential part of creative interpretation. It must, however, be allied to knowledge. Today we have better knowledge to help us to penetrate the feeling of a play of the past than was

M

available to our predecessors. The science of archaeology is vastly developed since the actors of the early Renaissance attempted to play the comedies of Plautus and Terence or, indeed, since Charles Kean and his fellow actor-managers tried to give archaeological realism to the plays of Shakespeare. We have a wide and intense concern with social history, and, in the field of theatre history, we have the scholarship which stems from the research of A. C. Bradley and Sir Edmund Chambers and which is today embodied in the illuminating work of Allardyce Nicholl, Glynne Wickham, Richard Southern, and their many contemporaries. With their help we are able to obtain an extensive knowledge of past scenery, costumes, and theatre architecture. We can travel more feely and see the past for ourselves in the ancient theatres of Greece and Rome or in the court theatres of Drottningholm, Versailles, and Schwetzingen, whilst the discovery and interpretation of drawings, paintings, sculptures, inscriptions, and manuscripts are constantly shedding new light on past styles. We have university departments and faculties of drama—over five hundred in America alone—which can bring new scholarship to the study of style. We have extensive means for the communication and fertilization of ideas. With this background we can approach more closely to the style of a period than the actors of the eighteenth and nineteenth centuries, and our audience is more keenly aware of period style and more critical of its interpretation. But knowledge and feeling for past styles cannot alone provide the answer to creative interpretation. They are only the basis from which interpretation springs; there remains the all-important question of allying this half of the bridge with our contemporary shore—the techniques and taste of our age.

The artist is aware of contemporary taste and allies his production or performance accordingly; the great artist creates his own taste and persuades his public of its verisimilitude.

Visualizing the Play

Once the stage-artist has fully absorbed the feeling of the play he begins to visualize it. This visualizing process is an act of the imagination. Every stage-artist possesses in some form or another the ability to visualize a play when he reads it. To the director it takes the form of a vision of the whole play in action. This does not mean that he conceives a complete picture of every detail, but as he reads the play the characters begin to move, the text begins to take the form of acted speech, the background assumes a certain shape, the furniture takes up its position. To the actor the part he is to play begins to become a character and he to become that character. His observation of life, his past emotions become absorbed or drawn into it. The text takes spoken shape; it has a cadence, a rhythm, a tempo. To the scenic artist the background becomes a visual image interpreted in colour and form. In a series of lectures which I delivered at Bristol University, published under the title of *The Director in the Theatre*,[1] I spoke of this vision of interpretation: 'There is nothing mystical about this act of vision, most of us possess it in one form or another. When we read a book or a poem, or, sometimes, when we hear a piece of music, we conjure up a mental image of the characters, the landscape, the atmosphere, perhaps, of these things. Such mental images are first delineated for us by the writer, but our interpretation of them will be influenced by the things we our-selves have felt or seen, and each one will conjure up his own individual image.'

The danger of this vision that we have of a play in action when we read it is that we are inclined to see it before our senses have fully absorbed the feeling of the play itself and before we can apply sound scholarship to it. Imagination is inclined to jump ahead of reason and it is very hard to change the first vision we conceive in the light of later reason. The artist's impression of a play is in fact very important, it represents the impression the play could make upon an audience, but this impression should not be formed into a final interpretative shape until we have considered all the given circumstances of the play both from the point of view of its original style and of the conditions of its contemporary production. Imagination must not be allowed to play its part in creative interpretation until our reason is ready to direct it. Nevertheless, dangerous as the imagination may be if we allow

[1] Routledge and Kegan Paul, 1954.

it to jump ahead of our reason, there can be no creative interpretation without it. Critics who ask why the director of a
Shakespeare play does not let the play speak for itself are talking
nonsense. A play text does not speak for itself; it is written to be
interpreted, and it must be interpreted not only in all sorts of
varying conditions, but by all sorts of people to all sorts of people.
Not only do taste, feeling for style, and the given circumstances
of a particular performance condition the way in which a play is
interpreted, but above all the creative art of the director, actors,
and designer. If the playwright objects to creative interpretation,
then he should not write for the theatre.

The theatre must create if it is to remain alive; every interpretation of a play or a scene or a character must be freshly
conceived. The director, the actor, and the scenic designer must
treat the play as though it had just been written and yet—
and here is the seeming paradox—they must relate it to the style of
its own age just as firmly as they relate it to their personal taste
or to the taste of their period. Perhaps the failure of religious
ritual with which, as we have seen, the theatre is so closely
related, is when it fails to make a fresh impression on us; when it
becomes a dreary repetition of sounds and actions which fail to
arouse our imagination, and so fail to make us identify ourselves
with the action—for religion is, or should be, action—and the
Lord's Prayer and even the Litany should come to us as a revelation of truth sanctified by time, not ossified by tradition. So,
too, theatrical ritual must be a revelation and a creative action.
'To be or not to be' must both surprise us with its ever-new
thought, its revelation of Hamlet's mind, and sanctify us with its
eternity. This is the ritual of the theatre and creative interpretation must make that ritual both young and old at the same time.

Technique

Technique is the physical means by which the artist conveys his
feeling for style and his imaginative vision to his audience. Since
it is conditioned by current methods and concerned with the
human approach it is subject to the changefulness of taste and
belongs to its own age. This does not excuse the stage-artist from

studying the techniques of the past and in certain cases from employing them. In Restoration comedy, as we have seen, the acting technique of the period, or the nearest approximation we can make to it, is the only effective means of conveying the style of the plays, but in plays of more universal meaning the actor's technique is less limited and contemporary techniques can legitimately be applied to the plays of Shakespeare or of Sophocles without prejudice to the interpretation of their style.

In Restoration Comedy technique and style are interwoven; in the plays of Shakespeare they can be separated. But style controls technique and determines the limits of creative interpretation. Our error is to confuse the two or to allow technique to determine the style.

Today we are preoccupied with the study of the technique of acting as expounded by Stanislavsky. This we confuse with Stanislavsky's style of acting. Stanislavsky did not pretend to teach a universal style of acting, he set out to provide a codification in a logical form of the way in which the stage-artist can develop his mental and physical equipment. He listed the requirements of the actor and suggested exercises to develop these requirements. His system is comprehensive and from it has sprung a whole variety of practical training systems—the 'method' of the United States, the 'epic' techniques of Brecht, the stage-training of a host of schools and academies of dramatic art in London, New York, Paris, and other European cities. From this codification of technique the student of the stage will discover something, but never everything; for the skills of the stage artist are not only consciously developed, they are, more often than not, the action of the sub-conscious. Many of the best contemporary actors and actresses have never studied Stanislavsky nor any of the other methods, for the English translation of his first book, *An Actor Prepares*, was only published in 1936. The effect of this book upon many actors, whose training was not based upon it, is a proof of the basic validity of its content, and constitutes a reasonable criticism of the whole idea of a codified formula for an art. The older actor often rejects his system as being something which he knew about already and finds that his instinctive skill is embodied in a wordy and complicated terminology. Stanislavsky uses words such as 'the magic of' to explain the comparatively natural dramatic action of make-believe, and 'emotional memory' to explain the process by which an actor uses personal emotions from his past experience to apply to the emotional reaction of the character he is playing. Both these actions are sub-conscious—something the actor does without realizing it; and indeed this applies to most of the codification of an actor's thought process.

The danger of terminology of this kind is that it means one thing to one artist and not quite the same thing to another. Stanislavsky was fully aware of this danger. 'The actors carefully questioned me about the special terminology which was used by us during the study of the system. This was accompanied by one error on my part and on the part of the actors for which I am still paying, and heavily.' He then refers to the difficulty of obtaining precise meaning from words which set out to explain an emotional or mental process.

As a result of this misunderstanding of words and emphasis, a serious deviation from the Stanislavsky system occurred in the Method training in the U.S.A. This error is pointed out by Robert Lewis in his excellent analysis of Stanislavsky's system and its relation to the Method.[1] It arose through the gap in time between the American publication dates of Stanislavsky's two main books, *An Actor Prepares* in 1936 and *Building a Character* in 1949. These books were meant to be read together. The first book was mainly concerned with the internal process of acting, the second with the external process, placing particular emphasis on vocal training, the projection of the voice, and the tempo and rhythm of speech. The Method was intensely studied in New York, during the 1930's, mainly by the Group Theatre; and there arose in the U.S.A. a form of naturalistic speech which was lacking in dramatic expression and often inaudible. Thus the gap of thirteen years which separated the publication of the two halves of Stanislavsky's system gave rise to a mannerism which has often brought criticism upon American acting and accounts in

[1] *Method or Madness*, by Robert Lewis. Heinemann, 1960.

part for the failure of many American actors to master dramatic verse and the plays of the prenaturalistic tradition.

The error, then, is to confuse Stanislavsky's teaching with a particular *style of acting*. This confusion of technique with style is explained by the fact that his teaching is usually associated with the performance of naturalistic plays both in the U.S.S.R. and the U.S.A., but, in fact, Stanislavsky himself did not only present the plays of Tchekhov, Gorky, and Ibsen, but also plays of Shakespeare and Goldoni, and, at the time of his death, he was studying opera and ballet. In Moscow there is the Music Theatre of Stanislavsky, as well as the Moscow Art Theatre, and some of the best work in the Russian theatre results from the impact of his system upon the acting of ballet and opera. It is, however, true that he failed with his productions of Shakespeare, as he himself admits. This was due, not to a fault in his technique, but to his own preoccupation with the naturalistic style of performance and his failure—and the failure of his age—to recognize the importance of conveying the original style. Here again we can see the danger of the codification of technique, for different period styles require a different emphasis to be placed upon various aspects of technique. We have seen how in the Elizabethan Theatre action determined characterization, and how in the Restoration Theatre characterization was mainly concerned with stock characters; in the study of Stanislavsky's system, therefore, the actor must relate his technique to the style of the play and its period.

The danger of a too rigid application of any system is that it tends to become a fetish—a bible of acting, rather than a springboard for the development of the actor. The tendency to treat Stanislavsky's work as the final word on the art of acting is observable in the U.S.S.R., where there has been little sign of any developments in acting technique or, indeed, in the methods of performance for the past twenty years. A system is not intended to be the final word, but merely a disciplinary basis for development. But the greatest benefit of Stanislavsky's work is that it has created an awareness both in the public mind and in the actor's that the stage is an art and has, like all arts, a discipline.

Whilst every actor and director must, perhaps, find his own discipline and live by it, an awareness and recognition of the function and limits of creative interpretation in the theatre is required if the stage is to avoid the recurrent periods of degeneration and stagnation that have marred its development in the past. The significance of the contribution made by Stanislavsky's teaching lies in his courageous attempt to provide a philosophy of theatre. Today that philosophy may need revision and there is, perhaps, a need to broaden its basis in relation to earlier styles of theatre of which we are becoming increasingly aware, but the basic truths of acting which he illuminated have provided us with standards that may well act as a safeguard against wholesale vulgarization of the actor's art.

CHAPTER EIGHTEEN

THE PRACTICE OF THEATRE

HAVING examined the historical development of the theatre and considered some of the theoretical problems involved in its staging, let us look finally at its practice. Practice concerns both stage and audience, since no play is alive until it is in contact with an audience.

The process of preparing a play varies widely, depending on the circumstances of the production and the personal methods of individual director. Any examination of this process can, therefore, only be regarded as a guide; it cannot be regarded as a rule.

Analysis of the Text

We have discussed the necessity for a stage-artist to possess a feeling for a play and the ability to see it when he reads it. A third quality required by him is the ability to sense the emotions and thoughts that lie beneath its surface. The text of a good play provides within itself clues to its interpretation. The most obvious form of clues are the stage-directions, but these are by no means the most important. In the plays of Athens and the Renaissance, which were either rehearsed by the playwright or with his co-operation, stage directions were either non-existent or contained in laconic remarks such as 'Enter fighting'. The plays of some modern playwrights are elaborately decorated with hints and instructions to make them more easily appreciated by a reading public which lacks the ability to visualize a play and to sense its inner emotional content. This is most noticeable in the plays of Barrie and Shaw, where the stage directions are almost as explicit as the descriptions in a novel. The published acting editions of most modern plays relate all the movements of the characters and list the lighting cues, properties, furniture, and costumes, as well as providing photographs and ground-plans of the scenery used in the original production. The clues provided by this means are either useful or the reverse. Their danger is that they can never be completely comprehensive and they can discourage the stage-artist from seeking the clues for himself, so that his performance lacks freshness and creative force. But when we talk of the clues to interpretation contained in the text of a play, we are thinking of something deeper than stage-directions. We are searching for the inner reality of the action: the reason *why* a character thinks and behaves as he does and *what* he is thinking and feeling at any given moment. The test of the dramatic value of a play's text is the depth and consistency of this inner reality which motivates the thought and action of the characters.

Stanislavsky calls this the sub-text of a play. It is, in fact, the double life of the characters. In a naturalistic play this double life goes on behind the dialogue and so the sub-text is unwritten. In the last act of Tchekhov's *Cherry Orchard* Madame Ranevsky suggests that Lopahin should marry her adopted daughter, Varya. Lopahin agrees without enthusiasm and he is left alone with Varya.

Varya   (*pretending to look for something amongst the luggage*): It's strange, I can't find it anywhere.
Lopahin: What are you looking for?
Varya: I packed it myself, and I can't remember. (*A pause.*)
Lopahin: Where are you going now, Varya?
Varya: I? To the Ragulins. I have arranged to go and look after their house—as a house-keeper.
Lopahin: That's in Yashnovo? Seventy miles away. (*A pause.*) So this is the end of life in this house.
Varya   (*still looking amongst the luggage*): Where is it? Perhaps I put it in the trunk. Yes, life in this house is over—there will be no more of it.
Lopahin: I'm just off to Harkhov—by the next train. I've a lot of business there. I'm leaving Epihodov here—I've taken him on.
Varya: Really.

Lopahin: This time last year it was snowing already. Do you remember? But now it's fine and sunny. Though it's cold, to be sure—three degrees of frost.

Varya: I haven't looked. (*A pause.*) Our thermometer's broken.
(*A voice from outside calls, 'Yermonay Alexeyevitch!'*)

Lopahin (*as though he had been expecting this summons*): Hold on! I'm coming.
(*He goes out quickly. Varya sits on the floor burying her head in the luggage and sobs quietly.*)

This text has nothing to do with the direct proposal of marriage. It does not represent the intention or major thoughts of Varya and Lopahin, but is merely surface conversation which veils their real thoughts. The unwritten sub-text is what matters: the prospect that faces Lopahin of proposing to a girl with whom he is not in love; and for Varya the complex emotional reaction of a girl who knows that Lopahin does not love her, and yet who desperately wants to be loved. Two intentions are, therefore, going on at the same time, the external necessity of maintaining conversation and the internal intention which deals with the reality of their feelings. These two levels must be made clear to the audience, so that even in a remark such as 'Our thermometer's broken', we can see the reality of the sub-text through the formal reality of the text. In a play written in dramatic verse, the sub-text need not be concealed. In the plays of Shakespeare the double life of the characters is often expressed by means of soliloquy and cloaked by poetic imagery. When Macbeth prepares to enter Duncan's bedroom, he expresses his feelings in terms of a mental image—the dagger that he sees before him. His intention and the thoughts of his sub-conscious mind are expressed in soliloquy—a form which is denied to the naturalistic playwright. Yet, even the plays of Shakespeare have an unwritten sub-text which must be acted, as for example when Macbeth and his wife are confronted by the suspicions of Macduff after the murder of Duncan, or when Macbeth wishes Banquo's horses 'swift and sure of foot'. It is the actor's task to analyse the text and sense the sub-text so that he can express the full character, not merely the surface character.

From this analysis of *why* the character thinks, speaks, and behaves in the way he does, will follow the *way* in which he speaks, behaves, and reacts to the speech and behaviour of the other characters; thus a complete network of action and reaction is built up.

Preparation

Before the play is put into rehearsal a preliminary period of analysis and preparation will have taken place. The director will decide upon the style of his production; he will analyse the text, conceive his vision of interpretation, and plan the general movement; the scenic-artist, in consultation with the director, will prepare the designs for the scenery and costumes, and consideration will be given by both director and scenic artist to the main features of lighting in relation to scenery and movement. Furniture and properties will also be designed or selected and the actors will be allotted their parts. The selection of the actors, if they are not members of a permanent company, may take many weeks of auditions and readings to ensure a proper balance. The actors, at least the principal ones, will discuss the general shape of the production with the director and will learn his views about the broad lines of interpretation. If the actor is wise he will not, however, conceive any final vision of the interpretation of the character he is to play, for this will be discovered best in rehearsal, though he may analyse his part and prepare himself for it by acquiring a background of knowledge upon which he can draw when the time comes for him to build his character.

In the theatres of Eastern Europe, where ample preparation time is available, frequent discussions are held between the actors and director on the style and analysis of a production, and no physical rehearsals begin until these matters have been fully explored and discovered by all who are taking part. The scenic-designer, the carpenter, the property-master, the costumier, the 'effects' man, and the lighting expert take part in this process of preparation by discussion and attend as many rehearsals as possible; as a result a considerable unity of purpose can be achieved from the beginning.

The conditions of British and American theatre systems rarely allow for such comprehensive team work. The organization and financial limitations of our theatres preclude a long preparatory period. Discussions have to be reduced to a minimum and the onus of decision falls mainly on the shoulders of the director. Regrettably, too, there exists a gulf between the creative work of the actors and the craftsmanship of the stage workers. The carpenters, electricians, sempstresses, property makers, and stage-hands are too rigidly regarded as departmental workers removed from the main creative effort of the actors; this is more true of the freelance system than of the repertory system. Lack of contact between craftsmen and actors leads to lack of a truly harmonious growth. However thorough the preparatory work of the director and designer may be, it can never be comprehensive; for the production of a play is an organic growth in which the constituent parts react in contact with each other. Differences of opinion and outlook are a necessary part of this process of growth, and whilst it is the director's job to control and shape the growth according to his vision and interpretation, it is also his job to stimulate the thought of his team and to incorporate these thoughts into the growth of the total conception. Creative interpretation is best achieved by the inter-action of ideas from all sources.

Rehearsal—First Phase

The early stages of rehearsal should emphasize clearly the total vision of the production. This phase should be a period during which the director is predominant. At the first rehearsal the style of the production will be explained by the director in broad outline; the models of the scenery and the sketches of the costumes will be examined; the play will be read through by the actors; and, if it is a new play, the playwright may explain his own views on the text and its interpretation. If time permits the early rehearsals will be concerned with reading the play several times. In the course of these readings the director will endeavour either directly or by stimulating discussion to bring out the play's meaning and the broad aspects of character analysis. Whilst it must be borne in mind that there are a variety of views on how to handle the early stages of rehearsal, the principle should be to restrain the actors from forming their vision of characterization too hastily. Jean Vilar, one of the foremost modern French directors and actors, has emphasized this point in his book *De La Tradition Theatrale*[1] 'A third of the rehearsal time should be given to word rehearsals, what we call "repéter à l'italienne". When you put an actor on the stage too quickly, his physical reactions are too hastily provoked.'

A third of the rehearsal time is probably too long for most actors to spend reading a play without causing a sense of frustration. The actor approaches his part more from the physical, than from the consciously intellectual, standpoint. He works best in movement, and it is by his physical action—his stance, movement, gesture, position—that his relationship with the text is established, but if these physical reactions are too hastily provoked false values are developed before the actor has had time to know what his mental attitudes and relationships should be. It is in the reading stage that the broad lines of character development and relationship are established and the whole effect and meaning of the play is discovered. During these readings, therefore, the director should endeavour to stimulate discussion and discovery, so that the broad aspects of character and the full implications of the play as a whole are understood.

As the readings proceed the actors begin to visualize themselves in motion and this visualization process takes physical form. The director will observe how an actor begins to want to act his part; he will want to get up from his chair and change his position, he will light a cigarette, turn himself this way or that, use gestures and tones of voice that intimate proximity or distance from the person he is addressing. From these indications the director will assess how the actor sees himself in action; as a result the director may decide to change the movements he has noted in his score, or, if he thinks the actor is wrong, he may correct his visualization before it becomes set. Readings are, therefore, invaluable both to the actors and to the director since it is easier to adjust the balance of a performance before physical factors are introduced than it is once action is established.

[1] L'Arche (Paris, 1955).

Rehearsal—Second Phase

The readings of the play will be followed by the arrangement of the actors' movement and groupings on the stage. This process of choreography is called 'blocking' in America and 'placing' in Britain. Here again the director should emphasize the total vision of the play, rather than a detailed one. For this reason it is desirable to place, however roughly, the moves of the whole play at once, rather than concentrate on reaching perfection in each scene. In this way the actors will have a general understanding of their total movement and of their general relation to each other and to the scenery. The principle sometimes adopted of rehearsing each scene or act in detail before passing on to the next can lead to a spasmodic process of characterization by the actors, who will tend to study the early manifestation of their characters unrelated to their final development.

Some directors prefer to come to rehearsal with a fully prepared 'prompt-script' or 'score' of their production in advance. In this score the director notes down movement, gestures, music and 'effects' (or noises off-stage), and lighting changes. An example of such a score can be studied in Professor Balukhaty's *'The Seagull' Produced by Stanislavsky*.[1] Other directors prefer to come to rehearsal with no fixed movement in mind other than entrances and exits and a general arrangement of key positions. In general it can be said that the best preparation by the director is that which fully explores the play's style and analyses its text, whilst leaving latitude for development of characters and movement in rehearsal.

Rehearsal—Third Phase

Once the play has been visualized as a whole both in analysis of the general aspects of character and in inter-relationships between the characters, detailed rehearsal of each scene can proceed. This phase should be accompanied by a gradual withdrawal of the predominance of the director. His task is now to watch and guide the gradual growth of the actors' characters and to co-ordinate these characters with each other. The play is still kept within the framework of the director's vision, but within

[1] Dobson, 1952.

that framework the actor must be able to manœuvre freely. The dictatorial director who tries to impose his will on the actors will frustrate the creative effort of the actor. Gordon Craig advocated a type of super-artist who maniupulated his actors like marionettes; yet, in practice, Craig himself was an actor and would have been the last to submit himself to super-direction. The actor must be free to develop his character within the framework and unity of the whole, and, providing he has fully absorbed the framework, understood the reason for it and agreed with its principles and structure, he will find a way of expressing himself within it. The director's task, therefore, is to create the conditions of freedom whilst maintaining unity of style.

It is a common error of young directors to compose an inflexible pattern of movement and groupings at the beginning of rehearsals and to refuse any departure from it. Movement and grouping are, of course, important, just as important as composition in painting—a single move can change the balance of a phrase, as well as change the visual concentration of the audience—yet it is undesirable to fix these points of emphasis too definitely until the actor has had time to find his own points of emphasis. One of the main lessons of play-direction is to have confidence in the actor; to trust his intelligence, sensitivity, and professional ability. The composition of effective grouping and the highlights of movement can all be done quickly enough with the co-operation of experienced actors, once they have discovered their own way of playing their parts.

During this third phase the director must encourage the actor to find his own points of emphasis, both his physical and mental approach to the part. It is vital, therefore, to stimulate an atmosphere of liveliness and a sense of discovery during rehearsals; the director must never allow rehearsals to be boring. A mood of excitement generates creative imagination and encourages actors to make their full contribution to the composite art of creation. No director on the British stage knows better how to keep his rehearsals alive than Tyrone Guthrie. In his book *A Life in the Theatre*,[1] he asks the question, What makes a good director?

[1] Hamish Hamilton, 1960.

What matters is this: can you make a rehearsal into a lively experience for those who take part? Can you feel the material growing and taking shape and beginning to live as you and your collaborators work?

Rehearsal—Fourth Phase

The final phase of rehearsal will be reached when each scene has been studied and rehearsed in detail; when each actor is sure of what he is going to do and has started to do it. Then come the full 'run-throughs' of the play—act by act to start with, the director giving notes and making adjustments at the end of each act. Later the whole play is rehearsed straight through with the director's notes at the end. During this phase the actors form the total conception of their characters and develop them logically through the play. The director has now become their audience rather than their mentor. His notes on their characters are in the form of suggestions on how to make the actor's meaning more explicit to the audience.

Finally, costumes, scenery, and lights are added in the dress-rehearsal phase. This is a period that is seldom free from tension. Too often the various components do not unite in the way they had originally been planned. The music and effects are too long or too loud; the actors' positions do not coincide with the lighting; the costumes restrict movement and seem to dwarf the characters, or to express different characters to the ones built up in rehearsal. Unless the actor has been able to rehearse frequently in his costume or in a costume resembling the ones he is to wear, he is likely to find it tells against him at the last moment. Unless, too, he has been able to rehearse with elements of the scenery—especially with varying levels, steps, doors, and windows—as well as with music and effects, his performance will inevitably be thrown out of balance when he is introduced to them.

A wise director is constantly reminding his actors of these other elements of a production from the beginning of rehearsals and a wise actor is constantly taking them into account; visualizing the effect of background music, a gradually darkening stage, the distant noise of a train, for such effects will condition his own

N

performance; they may alter his tone of voice or radically change his mood; they may effect his rhythm and pauses or control his position and focus. An experienced actor is also aware of audience reactions, for no matter how naturalistic his approach to a part may be, he still requires to understand and allow for the reactions of those to whom he is interpreting it. A laugh in the wrong place can destroy the whole effect of a carefully built up scene, but even more difficult is the understanding of how to get a laugh in the right place, for comedy makes greater demands on an actor's experience of audience reaction than tragedy, though tragedy, too, requires an understanding of audience psychology. The darker the tragedy the more difficult it is to play, and the Elizabethan and Jacobean tragedies, where corpses mount up in the final scenes and little relief is supplied to the dramatic tension, can prove intractable so far as involving the audience in the action is concerned.

In the preparation and rehearsal of a play the reason and imagination of the stage-artist are required to work in harmony. Imagination is his greatest inspirational force, whilst reason working through his technique should shape and guide his creative power, so that his performance is not only a truthful interpretation of the play's text, but is explicit to the audience. For the final and only real test of a play is its impact on an audience.

The Final Phase—The Play and the Audience

Audiences vary from age to age, from place to place, and even from night to night. An actor's first question to his fellow actors who have preceded him on to the stage is nearly always, 'What are they like out front?' A good actor reacts to this mood 'out front' and adjusts his performance to suit it. This does not mean that major alterations should take place, but the actor must always maintain a degree of flexibility to command attention. Flexibility is mainly confined to slight variations of vocal projection and tempo. With a practised team this flexibility will be a concerted effort, so that no actual disturbance is caused to the unity of the whole. Final stimulation comes from this contact with an audience. It is the audience which brings the play to life or which kills it. Thus, a play is never static like a film or a television drama, for always there is a second force present—the live audience.

The Making of an Audience

For good theatre it is just as necessary to have a good audience as good actors. Whilst the critic, the theatre historian, and the growing number of actors and directors who write about their work can contribute to the creation of an appreciative and well-informed audience, it is only by seeing good theatre sufficiently frequently that sound judgement is formed. By good theatre is meant not merely good performances but a well-balanced and representative repertoire. In Germany, Holland, and Scandinavia every town of moderate size supports a well-housed municipal or state theatre, unfettered by political ideologies and sufficiently subsidized to enable the public to see plays selected for their artistic merit rather than for their commercial or political advantages, at prices which are within the means of all. As a result there exists in these countries a wider appreciation of theatre than in Britain and America. This pattern is gradually changing, and in Britain the larger repertory companies, aided by the Arts Council, have done much to encourage the appreciation of their audiences for a wider range of theatre, but lack of sufficient subsidy restricts a full development, and often unattractive and inadequate theatre buildings provide small inducement to theatre-going outside London. Perhaps the main reasons for the reluctance of our civic authorities to provide the public with first-class theatre is, first, an inherent distrust of the stage as an art, which still lingers on in the remains of our Puritan conscience; and secondly, the heritage of nineteenth-century commercialism which still causes us to regard theatres as a business enterprise which ought to be making profits.

Theatre is a service to the community as vital to the life of society as the services of libraries, museums, art galleries, the radio and television. Whilst profit-making need not be divorced from it, it must not be regarded as a motive for it.

A liberal society which has discarded the doctrines of religious and political conformity must accept responsibilities if it is to safeguard the right to preserve its liberties. A liberal theatre is not required to conform to a single ideology nor to express itself in terms of a uniform motive, but the profit-motive ties the theatre to a materialist ideology resulting in a narrow form of theatre and exposes it to the worst excesses of vulgarity.

The responsibility of society towards the theatre will be conditioned by a respect for its values. These values—the enrichment of our experience and the particular pleasure that is derived from participation in a living art—must be demonstrated in conditions which earn the public's respect. Upon the acceptance of this responsibility by the managements and patrons of theatre, no less than by the stage-artists, depends the very existence of the live theatre.

INDEX